Snow White and the Savage 2

Fatima Munroe

A Word...

Actually a warning: if you've read my work in the past, you know I don't write predictable books. Snow White and the Savage 2 isn't a typical happy ending like the original Disney book. You get to see the depth of these characters as they go through their ups and downs, as well as secrets being revealed.

In this book, I have a few surprise guests. If you've read the Married To A Chicago Bully series and the spinoff, Trapped In My Feelings by a Chicago Boss, you're pretty familiar with Atif Hermes. I couldn't write a Miami book without him somewhere in the mix, so...wait. I almost told the book. If you haven't read these three books prior, go ahead and get caught up.

Married To A Chicago Bully (two book series): https://amzn.to/2uWoyAs

Trapped In My Feelings By A Chicago Boss: https://amzn.to/2sAmEE1

By the way, Cary wanted me to recommend this to y'all: https://amzn.to/2DnfPOj

What's coming from Monreaux Publications, you ask? Click here: https://bit.ly/MonPub2

Regardless of how this book makes you feel, please leave me a review if you enjoyed! I read them all!

Keep scrolling at the end for a blurb from my next book (which will be exclusive to my website), Enigmatic.

Join my reading group so we can chat about THIS one though: http://facebook.com/groups/ReadingWithFatima

Fatima Munroe

Table of Contents

Synopsis

Miami's favorite princess has grown into a queen in her own right, and all is wrong in the kingdom. At the end of book one, Cary was kidnapped from her own home by none other than her wicked stepmother Lenore, who is still determined to sit on the throne she feels she helped to build. But when Juelz sends a God to her rescue instead of a king is when all hell breaks loose.

Hailing from the streets of the Chi, Atif moved to Miami and gave up the game when his wife died. Although he found solace in his new wife Royalty for a while, Atif's interest is piqued when he does a favor for an old associate and finds himself face to face with Cary. What's a man to do when he's tasked with the decision to stay with the rebound chick or follow his heart?

When Cary discovered that Leonidas hadn't truly broken things off completely with Okeema, leaving was her only option. Ever since he came to her rescue, the savage who the streets called God was determined to have her call him Atif while she screamed his name. Time and time again, he showed her who he was, all she had to do was let down the walls around her guarded heart. For all their good and bad times, was she ready to give up Leonidas to get her happily ever after?

An indecisive queen who has to make a choice between a king and a God…who wants that perfect love story anyway?

"CARY!"

I turned the water off and searched through the cabinet for my body oil. Aunt Maggie sent me something from Brazil that she said would work wonders on the eczema flare-ups I got from time to time. "What?"

"Get dressed. We gotta get down to the docks and find out what the fuck is going on!" Leonidas spat angrily.

"What are you talking about? What happened?"

"Lenore's ass is gone!"

"Gone? How?"

"I don't know, but we both know the first place she gonna pop up at."

"FUCK!" Every time. Every fucking time I found a corner of happiness, this happened. First she took my daddy from me, now it looked like she was trying to take Leonidas from me too. "We gotta get out of here before she—"

I damn near jumped out of my skin when someone started beating on the door out of nowhere. Leonidas grabbed his pistol from the dresser and stormed through the condo to answer it. "WHO IS IT!"

"Maintenance."

"Oh, I forgot I called them earlier." I pushed past him to open the door. "They came to take a look at the garbage disposal, it's making some kind of noise." I slid the chain from the door and unlocked the knob.

"Cary, don't—"

"What? It's just the—" was the last words I said before somebody kicked the door in and a hand wrapped around my throat.

"You an' this nigga thought y'all was gon' run me outta Miami, huh," Tony growled, yanking my head through the door. "When I say move, you move! When I say stay, you stay, dammit!"

"King, I see you've met my nephew," Lenore's voice grated my nerves every time I heard that presumptuous alto of hers. "Since your mother is gone, looks like we're going to become one big, happy family once this lil' hoe pays me what she owes me."

Tuh. Lenore really think I'm out here pussy after all she put me through. Somebody should've told her how I did Myron and Kimoyrah. That's ok, she'll find out the same way they did.

Chapter 1

Leonidas

Soon as she started unlocking the door, I got sprayed with mace as Lenore and Cary's ex nigga snatched my baby from me a second time. Reaching for my pistol with the chemical still burning my eyes, Cary's well-being was the first thing on my mind. Blinking like hell, I wiped my eyes with one hand while aiming at the light skinned blur in front of me with the other. Half blind, I started shooting before the beige blob shifted to the chocolate that I knew all too well. Lenore and her nephew was some grimey bastards, shielding themselves with my girl. I stopped shooting and started swinging as they moved down the hall towards the elevator. "CARY!"

"LEONIDAS! Don't let her—" her voice faded down the hall as I heard the elevator doors open and close.

‡

I got back to her spot and washed the rest of the chemical from my eyes. Pop had to give me some answers, way more than that vague shit he been pulling these past couple of weeks. Even with his wife gone, he still tried to flex like he didn't know what the hell was going on. Low key, he was pissing me off but Cary gave me a reason not to dig deeper. Now that she was gone, though? And the bitch he was cheating on my mother with was the one who snatched her?

• • •
13

Nah, this nigga owed me some answers. And I knew exactly who to call to get them too.

"Benny, what's good my G? You at the spot?"

"Shit." This nigga sounded like he was just getting up and it was damn near one o'clock in the afternoon. "I can be, what's going on?"

"Cary. That bitch Lenore—"

"Say less, I'm on my way."

Regardless of what him and Cary went through, I could still depend on him to pull up when I needed. They say blood is thicker than water, but for us the hood was thicker than every muthafuckin' thing. I changed my shirt, grabbed my phone and money clip, then shot Jaden a text to track her phone. If he couldn't track her, then he needed to dump Pop's phone for his bitch phone number and track that hoe. Either way, I was getting my baby back and if a pussy ass hoe had to die in order for me to get her, then fuck it.

Chapter 2

Cary

"Fuck you thought you was goin', coming all the way out here to fuckin' Miami? Huh?" Tony sneered in my ear while Lenore talked that cash money bullshit to Leonidas about me. How this hoe thought I owed her anything other than a foot up her ass was beyond me, but I let her have her little moment or whateva. "You don't move unless I tell you to! You don't breathe unless I tell you to! You don't leave the damn state without checking in with your owner first! And I didn't give you my permission to go no damn where!" he spat.

I saw Lenore reach into her bag and pull out a small canister of mace, spraying the thick liquid at my man while Tony's bitch ass pinned my arms to my sides. And just like I knew he would, Leonidas let out a pussy dripping roar before aiming his pistol and pulled the trigger. Lenore grabbed my arm to use me for a shield after those first two bullets whizzed past her ear, and Leonidas dropped his gun, still rubbing his eyes. Tony dragged me down the hallway with his funky ass hand over my mouth and I bit the shit outta him. Just as I heard something crash into the wall, I heard him yell my name. "CARY!"

"LEONIDAS!" I shouted as Tony stabbed the button for the elevator. From my peripheral vision, I saw Lenore heading towards the fire escape. That bitch wasn't gonna get away with this whether she walked, jogged, or ran out of my building. "Don't let her—"

Tony shoved me into the elevator and smacked the button for the doors to close even after they did. "I should make you get on yo' knees right here in this elevator!" he snapped.

"Try it and see what happen," I challenged. "I'm not the same Cary that left yo' dumb ass in Mississippi with yo' bad ass kids and that trash bag wife of yours!"

"Show how much you know, bitch I ain't even married!" he cackled.

"That's cap like a muthafucka!" I cackled with him. "That sour patch pussy hoe came with you to the company picnic! And I saw her driving your truck more than once!"

"My baby mama got some good pussy, but yours is way better," he whispered harshly in my ear. "You blocked my number, I told you I got eyes on you wherever you go! Fuck was I supposed to do, Cary! Huh! Fuck was I supposed to do without you!"

Tony grabbed my neck and I lost it, using all my strength I shoved him into the back wall just as the doors slid open. I ran out the elevator first while he was still trying to catch his breath. Lenore popped up out of nowhere with a stun gun in her hand and shot one hundred and ten volts of electricity through my arm. I felt each volt as my legs gave way and I hit the floor with my muscles still seizing from the shock. "Where do you think you're going, lil' bih?" she stood over my body to taunt me.

"I know where she goin'." Tony picked me up bridal style and carried me to an unmarked truck parked in front of the building. Dumping me inside like a bag of old clothes, that sick bastard ran his hand up my thigh while I was paralyzed and probably in shock. "I'ma be nice this time an' not put my dick in yo' mouth because I don' want you to bite my shit. You gonna give me some pussy though," he growled in my ear while Lenore drove.

With the electricity still gripping my nerves, I couldn't speak, but watching as he hovered above me and started unbuttoning his pants, I willed myself to do something to protect Cary Muhammed. In the muted light of the van's interior, my mind went back to that day on that bathroom floor all those years ago. I was mad. I was fucking mad. "Nnnn…nnnn…"

The van suddenly dipped into a pothole as Lenore floored the vehicle on our way to God only knew where. "FUCK!"

"Watch where the hell you goin'!" Tony snapped to his…aunt? To be an 'only child', which was the lie she told my father, she shole had a lot of nieces and nephews. No wonder that hoe hadn't died, she multiplied. "Now where were we? Yea, you was about to give daddy some…"

And that's when it clicked. Fear took a back seat when my instincts kicked in, I kneed Tony in the dick and when he doubled over I head butted his ass. Grabbing the tire iron from near the back door, I smacked Lenore in the back of the head and the van swerved into a curb before crashing into a brick building. I hopped out, thankful that I was able to walk away from these two crazy muthafuckas without a scratch on me, and started running. My phone was in Tony's pocket, and I'll be damned if I went back for it.

Jogging down the street a little, I tried to stay incognito when I realized something. We were on my old block. I used to live down the street, me and my daddy. As long as I had been back in Miami, it never dawned on me to actually drive past 15727 Sunset Grove Lane because of the memories that came with it. I got to my old house and it didn't look as if anything had changed. Everything looked exactly the way it did the night the coroner rolled my daddy's body out of our home and into the black unmarked truck. Right down to the…curtains.

There was mail still in the box, and I had to know. Pulling the envelopes out of the receptacle, I flipped through the letters in complete shock. Lenore was still living in my house. The house she had my father murdered in. And according to the tax bill from the city of Miami, the house that was in BOTH of our names for some odd reason. Leonidas's words came back to me from the day I found out they called my father's war cabin 'the factory'. I'd just finished branding my first initial on Myron's forehead when he spoke up behind me:

"Remember when Auntie Maggie taught you that move?" He snickered at the agony in Myron's eyes as I kicked his naked body to the ground.

"Yea, but we were out here practicing on watermelons and shit." Benny handed me a machete and I debated on whether or not I wanted to castrate this man. In the end, I saved that for right before I stopped his heart. "Shoulda' been using live targets."

"Man, I love this cabin," Leonidas's tone was wistful as he reminisced on our childhood. "So you cool with us keeping it like this, or nah?"

"Why would I care what y'all did with this cabin? Didn't Daddy give it to Uncle Juelz?"

"Nah, this still yours."

"Even after all these years? I thought Lenore sold all my property."

"In order for her to sell this and anything else that your father bought, she'd have to prove you were dead. Since she didn't, she couldn't."

"That bitch sold my yacht though," I snapped as I used a hammer to smash Myron's knuckles one by one. "I'm still mad about that."

"She already had that deal in place before Ahseir died. When the buyer found out his signature was forged on the boat, he disappeared."

Myron's muffled screams made my nipples hard, and coupled with the fact that I just found out I was still a millionaire…shit, I was ready to fuck. "So you mean to tell me she didn't sell my house?"

"Not that I know of."

"I'ma have to go over there to see what's up then," Myron let out a bone chilling scream like the hoe he was when I separated his little dick from his body, and I smiled at his wife when I put the bullet in his brain so she knew she was next. "Benny, I got one for the concrete!"

All this time we been looking for her, she had us going around in circles so she could come back to my house and continue to live the life my father gave her while I had to put up with her nutty ass nephew for the past couple of years. Tuh. If it wasn't before, it was definitely personal now.

Chapter 3

Lenore

Word got back to me about Myron and Kimoyrah missing, and since Cary was back I put two and two together. I knew I needed to pop up in the city and let this hoe know who the reigning queen of Miami actually was. Every time I talked to Juelz, he bragged on that lil' dirt colored bitch that Christina birthed and Ahseir gushed over every day of her life. No matter what I did, he was always putting her wants and needs first and I didn't like that one bit. The only thing I could do that she couldn't was fuck her father, and I rode that dick every night screaming at the top of my lungs so she knew I had a piece of her father that she never could.

Ahseir was a good man, and had I not killed her, him and Christina probably would've had a beautiful life with their daughter. I saw him first though, and the bitch I called my best friend knew I wanted him. But no, she sat at the bar and they kept exchanging glances while I sent him drink after drink. Finally, when I decided to go shoot my shot, it was too late:

"So you gonna keep ignoring the drinks I keep sending you, huh." I plopped down on the bar stool next to where he sat babysitting the three shots of bourbon I already bought.

"Oh, I'm sorry, are you my secret admirer?" he smiled politely enough. God, he was even sexier up close.

"I am. What's wrong, you don't like free drinks?"

"I don't have a problem with free drinks, I just don't drink bourbon, that's all." He handed the bartender a napkin and the man disappeared. "I'm more of a rum drinker myself."

"Rum, huh." I got the bartender's attention while he and Christina were in the middle of a conversation that had her cheesing from ear to ear. "Excuse me, can you swap these for some…what's your preference?"

"Uhhh…anything aged at least twelve years should be fine," he waved me off and fixed his attention down the bar at my friend. "I noticed you talking to her, she married or y'all on some girls night out shit?"

"I uhhh—" I glanced down the bar at her black ass skin tone. Christina always thought she was too good to strip, but she ain't have no problem coming up here to watch me take my clothes off for money, talkin' bout she needed some tips. And every time I noticed one of these tricks that could possibly treat me to a better life, her crunchy ass would pop up outta nowhere blocking. This time though, she wasn't gonna be the reason this beautiful man slipped through my fingers. "…yea. She's married."

"Too bad." The bartender came back with his drink and he threw the liquor back before signaling for a double shot. He checked his phone real quick before switching his gaze to my face. "What about you? You married?"

"Nah, I'm free as a bird," I smirked. "What about you?"

The bartender sat a shot glass down in front of him and he threw it back similar to the first one, then gripped the biggest dick I ever seen in my life. "I wanna fuck."

"Lemme go tell her I'm leaving and—"

"I'll be outside. Have yo' ass out there in two minutes or I'm gone," he grunted, tossing a hundred dollar bill on the counter before he walked out.

I looked back and forth between his retreating figure and Christina, waving goodbye to her before I followed him out the bar. We drove to the alley behind the bar and he put that tree trunk in my lungs until I couldn't take it anymore.

After that first night, we would meet up after I finished my set to fuck. I didn't know nothing about him and Christina until I bumped into her at the mall and saw her belly poked out. When I asked who she was pregnant by, she admitted Ahseir had the bartender slip her his number and she called him that night. Listening to her gush about how good he treated her, how he waited until she was ready before they 'made love', how they'd been all over Miami going on lil' pussy ass dates and shit...I got madder and madder. Every time he left her, I got a phone call to meet up. This man couldn't take me to a hotel when he wanted to dig in my guts, it was always a quickie in a parking lot. And he held on to the condom to make sure it didn't slip off. But Christina…he gave her the muthafuckin' world according to her.

After that I started making plans. Since she had a high risk pregnancy, Christina asked me to be her child's godmother and I agreed. She always wanted to meet up and talk about her wishes in the event anything happened. When I would ask about whether or not her child's father knew I was the godmother, she thought it was better to wait until after she had the baby for us to meet, not knowing I was fucking her man faithfully. I learned as much about Ahseir as possible, and during her last trimester I put my plan in motion. She never noticed those three drops of Visine in her tea when she would go to the bathroom because that big headed daughter of hers was always laying on her bladder.

The day she died, we were having lunch at a restaurant on Miami Beach when she went into labor after guzzling down a cup of tea that I mixed with her special medication. I hadn't planned on it working so soon, and I was seriously trying to kill them both; her and that trifling ass baby. The restaurant staff called the ambulance when she fainted as we were leaving, and the hospital did everything they could to save her before she succumbed to her mystery 'illness'. Her death was so much of a mystery that I fucked the coroner and made sure her death certificate said she died of a sudden heart attack.

I was there to console Ahseir in the hospital while he mourned the love of his life and tried to celebrate the birth of his daughter. I helped Judy plan Christina's funeral because Ahseir was depressed, and I even babysat on the days when he could barely get out of bed. I gave him pussy when he wanted it, sat in the bed while he yelled at the top of his lungs about the hoe he lost, and allowed him to slap me across my face when he wanted to blame someone for her death because he couldn't fight God. So for all that I went through, damn right I deserved every penny I got from him alive and in death.

As good as the dick was, it wasn't worth me being a stepmother to that brat he called his princess. Don't get me wrong, I tried it out for nine years. But no matter how much Ahseir told me he loved me, no matter how much time passed, no matter how much Ahseir told her to call me mama, Cary's lil' uppity ass always called me by my first name. Not only that, no matter how hard I fucked her father, she still had him wrapped around HER little finger. The thought of having to deal with teenage Cary didn't sound like no fun shit to do, so once again I started making plans.

When he would run the streets with Juelz, I started going through his stuff. His will left everything to be split between me and Cary in the event of his death, and all his insurance paperwork listed me as the sole beneficiary as his spouse. The Dade County coroner I knew retired, and his replacement was a woman, so I couldn't kill Ahseir the same way I did his bitch. I met up with Juelz one night when I was mad initially to vent, like I always did. That particular night, all of a sudden he wanted to act like a dick, so I dropped a few Visine drops in his bourbon while his head was turned:

● ● ●

"Now what was you sayin' 'bout Ahseir?" Juelz, glared at me through vindictive slits after he waved a few men over to our table.

"I was sayin' that I don't know how to get through to him. Every time I think we taking two steps forward—"

"AYYYEEE, AYYYEEE, AYYYEEE!" one of the men bopped to our table with a drink in his hand as well. "Toast up niggas, we just cracked a milli on these hoes!"

Juelz threw his drink back and signaled for another one as he shook up with his crew. "What's good wit'cho, ma? You tryna fuck ta-nite?" he slurred.

Why not? If nothing else I could take that married dick on a test run and Judy would never know. Plus getting closer to him I could get a little better intel on what my own husband was doing. Juelz wouldn't remember anything tomorrow. "Yea, let's go."

I made a move to get up and he slammed a hand down on my shoulder so I wouldn't move. "Nah, you stay right here." He shooed the men out of the VIP area where we were and I hit record on the device in my purse. Most women carried a pistol, but not me. I overheard too much shit back when I used to work the strip clubs to not be in a position to blackmail a muthafucka.

"So you gonna rape me, Juelz? Knowing I'm Ahseir's wife?"

"You said you was tryna fuck ta-nite, I'm just giving you what you want," he snickered sickly, releasing his man pole from behind

● ● ●

the zipper. Damn, him and Ahseir both had some big, pretty dick. "Come suck a boss' dick for a lil' while."

My mouth watered as I accepted his meat between my cheeks, cupping his balls as I bobbed back and forth. "Mmm…it's so big, Juelz."

"Bigger than yo' husband, ain't it?" he caressed my face, then grabbed the back of my head and shoved himself down my throat. "He said yo' head game was good, lemme hit that pussy an' see if that's good too."

I slipped out of my panties and hiked the dress up to my waist. Juelz bent me over the table and shoved himself deep in my guts. "Lenore, this sum good pussy girl…"

"Lemme give it to you all the time," I wheezed from underneath his weight. "Kill Ahseir for me."

"Uhhh…I can't do that, bitch…come suck yo' pussy off my dick and I might give you somebody who can…" he grunted.

I hopped up and swallowed his sausage until he nutted down my throat, continuing to milk him dry even after the vein under his dick went soft. "You got that number on you or not?" I wiped my mouth with the back of my hand and waited. His speech was starting to slur, and I didn't know if it was the liquor, the Visine, or something else. He scribbled something on a napkin, and I got the fuck outta there before something happened.

It took me two weeks to decipher the number, but I finally got the hitman on the phone and told him what I wanted. The night he killed Ahseir, he was supposed to kill his lil' bad ass daughter too, but she disappeared. I would've found her eventually, but some damn body called the police. All these years I didn't know if it was her or not, but seeing her go to foster care, I didn't give a fuck.

When Ahseir died, he left an emergency stash of coke, heroin, and pills, along with some money in the safe built in the wall of our bedroom. I hooked up with his workers, gave them a sob story, and they got that work off for me in no time. Juelz tried telling me that wasn't how things ran on the streets, but when I replayed the recording from that night and told him I sent a copy of the tape to five people I knew, he left me alone. From that day to this one, I kept him in my pocket to do whatever I wanted, as long as he wanted to keep his lil' family intact.

I was floored when I found out all the paperwork in Ahseir's office leaving all his property to me when he died was a fucking lie. When I went to sell that house on Sunset Grove Lane, the tax office told me I couldn't because it belonged to Cary Muhammed. It ALWAYS belonged to Cary fucking Muhammed. Christina's name was nowhere on it, hell Ahseir's name wasn't on it. The lawyer I didn't know he had showed up at the house and told me legally the only thing Ahseir owned outright was a fucking yacht. His bank accounts, real estate…everything I thought he had was in his daughter's name. I knew I would look suspect if I killed her little ass too, considering that they were never able to build a case against me for Ahseir's death, and I was the last person seen with Christina before she died. Nah, I was too light skinned to go to prison.

With Ahseir dead, I had to switch up my original plan to get rid of Cary, but that plan was on a temporary hold once I got married again. Michael, my late husband, was an executive producer for some of Hollywood's biggest blockbusters and a few TV shows. I kept bumping into him all over Miami, so one day we decided to try out a friendship. Ahseir never paid me that much attention, and Michael would shower me with gifts just because. After my husband died, I went to Michael's house to mourn. One thing led to another, next thing I knew I was married again.

Considering how quick I was able to move the weight I had at the house, not to mention the fact that I was Ahseir's wife, I thought Juelz would allow me to move into his vacated spot. After all, their Dominican connect knew me, the men respected me, and it would have been the more logical choice. When I showed up at the warehouse near the water for the monthly meetings, I saw Leonidas sitting at the other end of the table across from his father. I was livid when he had me escorted out of the building, and replayed the tape from that night on his voicemail as I waited for him to call me back and explain himself.

Juelz never showed up but Donnell did, giving me a refill on the Quaaludes along with a few other medications. He gave me his number and told me to give him a call when I ran out. I became the connect when it came to pills, Juelz still ran the streets and I didn't give him a dime. He owed me that for convincing me to kill Ahseir and not giving me his spot at the table with the made men.

Even though I was married to a famous executive producer, I still wanted my own money. Hence the reason I put in my own work using my connections introduced to me by my new husband. Michael thought I was meeting up with those women to go shopping and to sip mimosas…nah, I was serving those hoes that pack. I had the play set up so pretty, I would've never left Miami had not one of those dumb bitches died from an overdose. I knew the cameras in her building saw me walk in, and once again, technically I was the last person to see her alive. Using my knowledge of how shit moved on the streets, I convinced my husband to move back to California and got back on like I never left.

‡

Juelz didn't conduct business at his home with just anybody; he had this thing about not giving niggas the opportunity to take over what he built right under his nose. So when I showed up at his house that day with my niece, of course he was shocked. But since I was back, I refused to go through the same thing I went through with Ahseir when we met. Juelz wasn't gonna be fucking me in parking lots or back alleys, as the widow of not only his best friend but also a celebrity, I was worth a lot more than that.

After that little snafu with his kids and that lil' Cuban bitch, I figured I'd lay low. I knew he hadn't told his family about us, and since he seemed to be dragging his feet about divorcing his wife, I figured I'd give him a nudge. Okeema did whatever her auntie asked her to, so I told her to give him some pussy. Lately he had been acting as if he didn't care about the recording, so I needed something that would hold his attention until I came up with another plan. He had been acting stingy with that dick anyway, and I was overdue for another taste of him.

"Hey Juelz," I cooed into the phone's speaker after he called himself kicking me out of his home on the water. "I was just calling to let you know that I took care of your wife." I smiled to myself as I remembered the look on Judy's face when her limousine driver put a pistol to her head and told her to get out in the middle of the empty lot. Her wedding ring was in the shop, I had my jeweler filing off the inscription as we spoke.

"My wife? Fuck you talmbout 'you took care of my wife'?" he snapped.

"I told you when we first linked we was gonna be together, fuck you think I'm talmbout?" I shot back. Mel, one of my head honchos, sounded just like Juelz on the phone. So much so, his own wife couldn't tell that wasn't her husband with her dumb ass.

"Bitch I'ma fuck you up! I told you—"

"No Juelz, I told you! You not Ahseir! You ain't never gonna be Ahseir! And you and that Jamaican bitch ain't gonna ever be Ahseir and Christina! Stop calling that spoiled lil' bitch your daughter!"

"The only person who think I AM Ahseir is YOU! I'ma beat the fuck outta you if you don't tell me where my bitch at! Yo' muthafuckin' ass crazy!"

"You'll see things my way one of these days. Until then, fuck you an' that hoe!" I clapped back and hung up.

I had no idea where Judy was, all I knew was Tony said she wasn't underneath that house where my people stashed her body that day. Since Juelz wasn't looking for her, that only meant one thing: Cary's raggedy ass found her. This was the second time I missed that bitch, first time was when I blew up that restaurant of hers when Juelz called himself ignoring me. He was supposed to be bringing me some money, but at the last minute he decided to have some family time with his 'wife'.

After we hung up, I called Tony to strategize on how we were gonna snatch Cary up. As much as I hated her, she was also the key to me getting access to everything that Ahseir owed me, and I was past ready to collect. While we were watching Juelz's main trap house, that lil' bitch Mya snuck me and had me tied up while Tony went to take a piss. She threw me in the trunk where she already had Okeema gagged and tied up, then pricked both of us with the same needle. We woke up at a rundown house in Overtown with her waving a pistol and talking gibberish.

I wasn't surprised that she teamed up with my enemy, but I was upset that considering how much my niece genuinely cared for him, my stepson was in love with Cary. Always fucking Cary. I hated her for being the reason I was still coming up with plots and plans instead of living my life as a rich widow. Michael's first wife benefitted the most from his death. He conveniently forgot to change his will once we got married and California law gave her the bulk of his estate since they were been married a lot longer than me and him. All the hard work I put into those nail bars, used all my connections to find some good, quality women to strip…all that shit went down the drain when the lawyer read his will. I sat across the table staring at the woman who owned my livelihood and she didn't give me not one red cent.

That was my main reasoning for coming back to Miami. I hadn't been broke in a long time, but without Michael's money I wasn't living the life I was accustomed to either.
Everything…everything stemmed from Cary's legacy, from her mother stealing the life that should have been mine to Ahseir fucking me out of what I was owed as his wife and life partner. My plan was to torture that lil' hoe until she signed over everything to me that her father hadn't.

When I woke up in a cage on the docks, I prayed that Tony followed me. He waited a few days before he rescued us, and I cussed him out for that. He should have pulled up on us way before he did. I had Okeema tucked off at a house in Fort Lauderdale while I took care of Cary myself. Since Tony was just as crazy as me, I let him come with me to her house. Did I expect to get a pistol pointed at me? No. Did I expect Leonidas to punch a hole in the wall when I ducked because he swung at me? No. What he should have done was just let me take our bitch and leave peacefully.

I knew from the look in Tony's eyes when he laid eyes on her at her apartment that he was gonna try something, and adjusted the rear view mirror so I could watch. Myron did his thing with her while she was younger, and from the way he described it, I knew she liked it. Then when she started working at the truck stops, I knew I was right. I took my eye off of her for a second, next thing I knew I got hit with something hard and she disappeared. What Cary didn't know was that I'd blow Miami up if I had to before she'd ever receive any shred of happiness at my expense.

Chapter 4

Leonidas

"So, lemme get this straight: you lost Cary. AGAIN." Pop bellowed in my ear like I knew he would. I didn't see why he was so upset, considering he was the one who had her father killed and neglected to tell anybody he was fucking her stepmother.

"Look, I need you to come out here to the factory so we can figure out how to get her back. All that otha' shit you can keep," I snapped. She wouldn't have been in the situation in the first place if it wasn't for him tiptoeing around with known hoes.

"Oh, straight like that?"

"Pop." I ran a hand down my face, not in the mood for him to be going back and forth like I was one of those lil' niggas that worked for him. "You coming or not?"

"Hmph. Naw, I ain't coming. Figure that shit out ya'self, I gotta find out where the fuck my wife—"

"Ma left you! She don't want you knowing where the fuck she is! What is so hard for you to understand about that!" I roared. This nigga was delusional if he thought after giving the order to have her kidnapped, she'd come back home to lay up.

"I KEEP TELLIN' Y'ALL! I DIDN'T HAVE HER KIDNAPPED! Damn, what's so hard for YOU to understand! I told yo' mama she shouldn't have dropped you on yo' fuckin' head when you was a baby—"

"Nigga, you ain't nobody to fuckin' lie on! She don't want you, pussy ass hoe!"

"I'm still yo' fuckin' father, Leonidas! Yo' muthafuckin' ass betta—"

"Come do sumthin' bout it then! You know where I'm at, nigga get at me!" I snapped, hanging up in his face. I knew he wasn't gonna come out here because I asked, but if I threatened him he'd show up.

"Benny, you got the concrete ready?" I tossed the throwaway phone into the swamp and rubbed my hands together.

"Yup. Let me know what we out here doing."

I wasn't gonna put my father in concrete unless he started talking reckless, in which case I had no control over what happened. However, with Lenore watching the whole family, I didn't know if she was gonna show up with him. Or if she was gonna send someone with him. Pop was moving way too greasy for me, and I needed to stay one step ahead of whatever he had going on. Luckily, there was only one way in and one way out of the factory, and either way I'd know if and when somebody showed up.

Me and Benny stayed quiet, both lost in our own thoughts up until we heard a boat pull up. I waved him to the back while I tucked the pistol in my waistband and walked on the front porch. "Wassam, Juelz. What you doin' out here?" I smirked, lighting a blunt.

"Lissen, King." His walk was a lot steadier this time than it was last time he was out here. "I know you. I know you well. You came from my nut sack, so I probably know you better than you know yaself. Let's talk like men before one of us do something that we might regret, aight?" He held a hand out for me to shake.

I looked at his hand and back at him before waving all that peace treaty shit to the everglades. Walking back in the house, I plopped down on the couch and dumped the ashes from the cigar in the ashtray. "Where yo' nu-nu bitch at?"

"Son, I'm trying to tell you me and Lenore ain't never—"

"So you just gonna lie to my fuckin' face?" I snapped, slapping the PlayStation controller off the table. "Pop, you ADMITTED you fucked my old work! You ADMITTED you fucked this bitch! Now you talkin' bout what you ain't doing!"

"ALRIGHT, DAMMIT! YES! Yes I cheated on my wife! Yes I fucked yo' girl! You don't know what these hoes got on me, King! Every night I go to fuckin' sleep, all I hear is my voice...MY VOICE on that fucking recording giving Lenore the phone number to one of our hitmen! I close my eyes and see my top dog, my fuckin' ace, DEAD! In a fuckin' coffin! All ova' some pussy that wasn't even that good! I made a mistake! ONE FUCKING MISTAKE that cost Ahseir his whole life! His daughter growing up without her father…your mother would've pulled up with the guillotine because a machete wouldn't do what she needed done if it was me! You know what that feels like? For years…YEARS knowing I caused that man's death! And this hoe taunting me behind it? Purposely sliding her niece in front of you, knowing she was yo' type, then having the bitch come fuck me while I was drunk? I just got off the phone with that hoe, she knew what was up! I'm losing my family, my livelihood all over a bust down ass stripper!" he broke down on the couch with his head dropped in his hands.

"Pop—"

"I just want my family back, man," his shoulders heaved up and down as he spoke. "I just want my wife and my family back! I can't bring my mans back, but I can at least look out for his daughter…I just want my family back."

"Come on, man." I wrapped an arm around his shoulder, not sure of what exactly to do. I ain't gonna lie like I wasn't pissed, but Pop wasn't vulnerable with me like that either.

"King, I give you my word…my muthafuckin' word is all I got in this world," he sniffed. "I know it ain't an excuse, but I was…man, I ain't never been that drunk off no liquor in my life. I'm telling you, Ahseir sold pills and I think she was dipping in his stash. My right hand to God, I would've never done no shit like that sober."

"I believe you, Pop." Lenore a sneaky bitch, the fact that she knew Okeema was at my house and encouraged her to fuck my father and me the same day said a lot about her manipulation skills. She didn't have the lingo like that for a muthafucka to just go off of her word.

"Aye, so we bout to ride on these hoes or what?" Benny came from the back room on go, as usual. "I'm already sicka this Lenore bitch an' she ain't did shit to me."

"Speaking of which, how's Santiago?" Pop wanted to know.

"He good." I left it at that. Until Pop's story checked out, he was still a suspect. "Call Lenore and tell her to meet you at the house."

"Aight." He grabbed his phone and lined up the play. All I heard was yelling on her end about how that was all she wanted from him and he needed to apologize for calling her a bitch earlier. "Aye, if you don't know where Judy Payano is, you still a muthafuckin' bitch, hoe!" he snapped before he hit the speaker button by accident.

"It wouldn't matter to you where she at if you wasn't such a fuckin' liar!" she shot back. "You know you bought that house for me!"

"My wife bought my house! Ain't nobody got shit for you, thirsty bitch!"

"You an' Ahseir think y'all so fuckin' slick!" she snapped. "When Okeema drop that load though, we'll see who get the last fuckin' laugh!"

"Judy Denise Payano will, hoe! I don't own nothing," he chuckled slyly. "If I drop dead tomorrow, my kids don't get shit! They got they own money! My wife papered the fuck up, I gotta ask her for money! If Okeema is pregnant by me, you betta tell her to figure that shit the fuck out! Ju-Ju stingy like a muthafucka!"

"I HATE YOU, AHSEIR! I FUCKIN HATE YOU!" she screamed before the phone disconnected.

"Oh, sis still mad at unc, huh," I bussed out laughing at how she was screaming like a crackhead on the phone. "She need to go to therapy or something, get that hurt out her system!"

"Aye, you know what though?" Benny spoke up again. "I know where she at."

"How you know?" me and Pop wanted to know.

"Think about it. She still mad at Ahseir. Y'all said she can't do shit with his stuff because everything belong to Cary. First thing she start talking bout is what she bout to get when Keema drop that load? She at the old spot."

"What?"

"Look, y'all remember Ahseir's old address?"

"Yea, Sunset Grove Lane," Pop spoke up. "He was supposed to buy the house down the street from me when I bought my spot."

"Pull up. I bet both of y'all 5g's that's where she at," Benny thumbed his nose and sat down next to Pop.

"Aye, what you doin' out here, Benny?" It finally registered on his face that it was just me and Benny at the cabin. Pop knew what it was.

"O.G., you askin' the wrong questions right now. We gotta get the Queen back."

"Wait...King, you didn't tell me Lenore had Cary! SHIT!"

"What?"

"I gotta make another phone call...aye get me back to the car so I can get a signal," Pop grabbed his phone and beat us out to the airboat.

"You don't think I can handle this, Juelz?" Benny looked hurt and that shit was funny as hell.

"Nothing against you, I'm...we'll talk about it when we get back on land, aight?"

We hit the boats and sped back to where the cars were parked. Considering the fact that my team was made up of all killas, I wondered who Lenore knew and what that had to do with Cary. More important, who was Pop calling?

As soon as his feet hit the sand, he had his face to the phone.
"Yea, God? I need a favor."

Who…God? The fuck?

Chapter 5

Cary

My house. MY house. This bitch was living…breathing…eating…shitting in my fuckin' house. The house I lived in with my daddy. The house he bought for my mother when he found out she was pregnant with his first daughter. The house that somehow belonged to me and a hoe I didn't share a bloodline with. How the fuck does that even happen.

I had a mind to run back to that van and beat the shit outta her and that asshole. I didn't even have keys to my own mini-mansion, but the curtains were still up. Peeking through the windows, I saw she changed the furniture, but it was in the same spots as my old stuff. And I bet if I went upstairs to my old room, my closet would still have the $2.5 million dollars in the corner of my panic room that I left that night. Not only did Daddy have a phone in there, he also tucked my cut of the business in the closet every night. If he forgot at night, he came in the morning and went in my closet before he would wake me up. We were the only two people with the combination:

"Daddy, what…what's wrong?" I rubbed my eyes, trying to focus on his oversized frame coming out of my princess closet. The sun was just barely peeking through the blinds as he straightened up and wiped off the glitter from my fairy dress that always stuck to his face. No doubt he bumped into it again like he'd done so many

mornings before, and I would wipe the stray bits before he left for the day.

"Nothing's wrong, baby cakes. Everything's ok. How did you sleep?" He sat on the bed next to me and rubbed my hair.

"Good. Is Auntie Maggie coming over today?"

"No, your Aunt Judy will be here after breakfast. She'll talk to your tutors and take you shopping."

"Oh. Lenore must be busy again," I sulked, secretly happy that I didn't have to see her hideous face for the entire day. Daddy always asked me to give her a chance, but I overheard them arguing a few times about money. "That's horrible."

"You don't see that concerned though," he chuckled.

"I ain't. So...," I changed the subject, talking about Lenore irked my last nerve, "...since Auntie is coming over, can we going out on the boat today?"

"'We?' Who is we, Cary?" Daddy snickered, pulling the covers up right underneath my chin.

"Me, Leonidas, Alberto, Mya..."

"I don't care, but make sure you ask your aunt if it's ok," he smiled warmly. "I got some business to take care of today, be my sweet little princess, ok?"

● ● ●

"I got'chu daddy," I beamed happily. "We going on the boat...we going on the boat..." I sang as he pecked my forehead before leaving for the day...

"I knew you would come here," Lenore's shrill cackle shattered through the memories I shared of my daddy. "Princesses always think they daddy gonna come along and save them, don't they?"

"I don't need to be saved from a bitch like you," I seethed. "A can of Raid should do the trick, trick!"

"But you do need saving from the big bad wolf though, don't you," Tony came up behind me and moved a lock of hair from the base of my neck, I felt his tongue slither across my skin. "Mmm..." he moaned with his dick pressed against my back, "gimme summa that Goldilocks pussy."

Before I could use the training I learned from Auntie Maggie, he had a knife to my throat, dragging the serrated edges across my windpipe. "Listen to your stepmother, sweetheart," Lenore beamed. "You are going to go down to the courts and tell them that you want to contest your father's will. You WILL tell them that your father was senile and..."

"Senile? My daddy wasn't senile!" I spat.

"LIKE I SAID, you're going to tell them that you don't want anything your father gave you and you want me to have it!" she yelled. "All those years...your father owes me!"

"Owes you?" I cackled, this chick was definitely off her meds. "All that money you spent on all them niggas that Daddy didn't know about? All that money you spent shoving coke up yo' nose? All that money you spent on Dumb and Dumber?"

"Who you calling Dumb and Dumber?" Tony gritted in my ear.

"You an' yo' sister, Okeema," I smirked at Lenore with a sly grin. "Yea, Jaden told me you gave these two little bastards up because you was too busy selling pussy in the strip clubs to be anybody's mother! What type of sick bitch goes back and tells the kids that fell out of that pot of chili between her legs that she they fuckin' auntie!"

"I ain't have no kids!" Lenore screamed. "This is my nephew!"

"You ain't got no fuckin' siblings, bitch! You think ain't nobody did no research on you? Living in my fuckin' house, fuckin' my father, and you wasn't shit but a fuck!"

"He married me though, didn't he?" she snapped back. "Yo' daddy loved fuckin' me! He loved sticking his dick in every hole on me! Said ain't nobody ever fucked him like me, not even yo' black ass mammy! I'm glad I killed that hoe!" she screamed.

"Wait, you did what?"

"I KILLED THAT BITCH! Yea Cary baby, you got me to thank for you not growing up with yo' mama, I dropped..."

Lenore caught my right fist to her mouth first and I was about to follow up with my left when Tony caught my arm. Before I could react, he wrapped a hand around my throat and started squeezing as the sirens whined in the distance.

"Bring…that…bitch…in…the…house…" Lenore's voice came from far away as I slowly blacked out.

Leonidas

"Lemme get this straight: they call him God? Who the hell is he for anybody to be calling him God?" I questioned Pops as we rode out to the marina. What was even crazier was that we were supposed to be meeting up with him at Al Capone's mansion. Something about him being from Chicago and he was feeling nostalgic.

"Listen, son. For the most part, I know you can handle the business. Lenore is a special type of slimy bitch though," he spoke as we pulled up to the meetup spot. "Normally I can send you to handle shit, but this bitch got a grudge and she knows everything about me, you…the whole family. You see how she got to your mother."

"Yea, but I don't think…"

"You said yourself that you don't know how she was able to infiltrate the family like she did," he continued. "To tell you the truth, I don't know either. Ain't like we got no slimy niggas on the team, and we been switched up how we did business back in the day. So I gotta go outside the family to somebody who she don't know in order to get some intel on this hoe."

No matter how much I didn't like it, it made sense. Santiago was still wobbly from that night and couldn't give us any information on what happened, so this nigga God was our best bet. We got out the car and walked inside where a light-skinned Creole looking Arab sat behind a cherry wood desk blowing a cigar with some premium fuckin' dope. I ain't never smelt no shit like that. "Whaddup. God?"

"Good seeing you again, Juelz. You must be Leonidas." He stood and shook up with me, Pops and Benny. "And you are...Benny, right?"

"Damn Pops, you had to give him our whole life history?" I chuckled, looking back and forth between both men.

"Actually, I ain't tell him nothing about y'all. Some shit he just knew off rip." Pop took a seat in front of the wooden desk that sat in front of a floor to ceiling window facing the ocean.

God walked to the bar and fixed himself a double shot of bourbon to go with his cigar before he sat back down behind the desk. "Gentlemen. Let's have a smoke and a drink before we discuss the matters of made men."

Pop grabbed a cigar from the humidor and took God up on his offer. Me and Benny said fuck it and poured ourselves a double shot of Louie the 13th before taking a seat in the leather chairs strategically placed in front of the desk. I knew the reason we were here was a matter of life and death, but this dude God didn't seem pressed one way or the other.

"God, Leonidas and Benny don't know your back story, and you know in this business you can't trust everybody," Pop began as he blew a ring of smoke in the air.

"Of course." God inhaled and exhaled one more puff of that good dope before he tapped out the half-smoked blunt in the ashtray. "You ever been to Chicago, Leonidas?"

"Nah."

"Been out here 'bout five years now," he spoke solemnly. "Moved down when my second wife decided she was sick of the cold Chicago winters. I lost her right over there," he pointed to a spot on the beach.

"Lost her?"

"She died while giving birth to my son." He stopped for a second to stare at that spot, lost in his own thoughts. "Kapri was a good woman. You got a good woman, Leonidas?"

"Actually, I do."

"Treasure her. Keep her close to you at all times. Most importantly, love her with no regrets," he spoke quietly in remembrance. "But I'm sure Juelz told you this, right?"

"Yea, Pop schooled me."

"Good." He took a deep breath in and let it out slowly. "I stayed down here because I wanted to start new, start fresh. I caught a lot of bodies back home and didn't want that for my boys. The game ain't always set up for you to get out clean, sometimes you gotta decide on whether or not the reward outweighs the risk."

"That's facts," Benny spoke up from my left side.

"My last wife a rider though," he continued. "She used to be a head hunter back in Milwaukee, and I ain't talking bout sucking no dick either. Yea, I was blessed with Royalty after the fact, and she a good one too. Sometimes you lucky to have two great loves in your life, somebody that loves you and your kids like her own, but still respects the fact that you had a life before her, know what I'm talkin' bout, Leonidas?" He leaned forward and folded his hands on the desk in front of us, looking me dead in my eye.

God seemed like he was getting at something, but on my mama's soul I didn't know what he was talking about. "Yea…"

"With that being said, tell me more about your relationship with Okeema." This nigga God knew everything for real-for real.

"Pop, you…"

"Son, I swear on your twin sisters I ain't said nothing!" he threw his hands up defensively.

"Leonidas, I know things. I see things. I've moved around this city for the past five years, yet this is the first time you've heard of me," he took a sip of bourbon. "Let's cut the bullshit and get down to the reason you're really here."

"Damn," Benny snickered from my side. "Juelz, I see why you called this nigga now!"

"Okeema…"

"You know Lenore killed that first girlfriend of yours, right? What was her name…Miranda?"

"What?"

"Y'all got a crazy stripper running loose around Miami an' y'all out here drinking Louie the 13th and blowing dope with me," he sat back and chuckled. "At Al Capone's mansion at that."

I jumped up first, but Pop signaled for me to sit back down. "Who is this bitch Lenore for real?"

"I like bitches that's this kinda crazy," God leaned back in his chair and relit the blunt to take another puff. "What y'all need from her? Information? Or y'all trying to get Cary back?"

"So you know why we here," I rubbed a hand down my face trying to collect my composure. This nigga God talked in riddles, but he was on point. "Where she at?"

"Ahseir's house. She been there this whole time," he spoke nonchalantly.

"Both of y'all owe me 5 g's." Benny sat back in his seat smugly. "Told y'all that's where she was!"

"But why?" Pop wanted to know.

"Familiarity, for one. Why not go back to the place where you felt the most power?" God spoke. "Plus she feel like it's hers anyway. Feel like she shoulda' got it when ya' top dog died. What y'all gonna do about her kids though?"

"Her KIDS?" Pop choked on his bourbon. "What kids?"

"Okeema and Tony," he spoke pointedly. "Her kids. Come on, Juelz, you knew she was giving up that box while she was in the clubs! Couple of niggas you know her kids father." He toyed with the ashtray before tapping the blunt out again for a second time.

"Why don't you just take that whole thing to the face?" Benny questioned.

"I don't like being too fucked up," God revealed. "Just enough for me to talk shit to y'all before I send somebody out there to go get this girl from that crazy ass stripper that got you on the clock whenever she feel like it," he directed that last statement to Pops.

"Aye, I'on need no help getting MY girl back!" I slammed the tumbler on the table, heated. "That's my bitch, I ain't no fuck nigga! The fuck—"

Pop stood up to calm me down while this nigga God sat back and laughed in my face. "Juelz knew who to call. Why you think you sitting here now? Some things he let you handle, and some things he knows he has other obligations, so we handle. Calm down, I'ma make sure she get home," he snickered.

"What about Lenore?" Pop questioned, still holding me back.

"That's your headache, Juelz. I'll let you and these lil' niggas take care of that." He stood up and went to the bar, pouring himself another drink with his back to us. Shoving Pop off of me, I reached for my pistol and before I got a chance to point it at his head, he spoke. "Try it, lil' nigga. I ain't afraid to die. Trust that ya' girl's neck will be slit and you'll be dead before I hit the floor though." He clinked a couple cubes of ice into his glass before pouring himself another double shot.

"LEONIDAS!" Pop roared in my ear. "Put the gun down!"

"You just gonna let him talk to me like that! Like I ain't the king of Miami!"

"You just gonna come in my fuckin' house and ask for my assistance, then pull a pistol out on me like I ain't got snipers on the roof?" God spoke calmly. "Like your sister's shop ain't down the street from here? Like I can't make a phone call and that plane your other sister is on can't mysteriously malfunction? Like your mother is tucked safe in that house on Lago Vista Drive in Beverly Hills?" He leaned against the bar and swished his drink.

Pop shook his head for me to stand down and I did. "Aye, I ain't mean to come at you like that, but when a muthafucka come snatch your woman out the house and you don't know whether she safe or not…"

"Trust me, I know young nigga." He sipped his drink as he walked back to his spot at the desk. "Not only did a muthafucka come to my house and kidnap my girl while she was pregnant, they also snatched up my son. I damn near burned this whole city down. That's the only reason y'all still standing here after disrespecting me, because I know what's going on in ya head right now."

"Me and you more alike than I thought," I rubbed my chin, wondering if Cary was aight. The look on her face when I last saw her…that was that look I vowed she'd never have twice. "So how this whole thing work? You gonna call us, or…"

"I'll be in touch." He waved a hand, I guess to let us know we were dismissed. Pop stood up and they shook up while me and Benny hit him with a head nod. As we got back in the car, I heard Pop let out a long sigh before he hit the push button start.

"Aye, you aight?"

"Yea, I'm good." He started the car up and we started down the road on our way to drop Benny off to pick up his ride.

"Who is God?"

"Son, there's a few things you don't know about the business, and right now isn't the time for me to tell you." He spoke with a finality to his words. "As long as we get Cary back, everything else can wait."

"Aight."

"Since we on the subject though, lemme ask you something."

"What's on ya mind, Pops?"

"Your mother is in California? And you knew?"

Shit. "Huh?"

"Son, I know y'all mad at me, but damn. A man pour his heart out about how he missing his family an' you can't even tell me where my bitch at? That's fucked up, don't you think?" he continued.

"Ma ain't no…"

"Aye, don't start that 'my mama ain't no bitch,' shit," he grumbled. "I know she ain't, I'm jus' sayin' I miss her. I understand your sisters not giving me her info, but you? King, you my son!"

My loyalty would always be with Ma Dukes, but he was my father. "Look Pop, once Cary come home, I'll give you her information, aight?"

"Aight, bet." He smiled to himself as he drove. Damn I hope I ain't making the wrong call, Ma gonna kill me.

Chapter 6

Cary

I was laying on the floor bound and gagged when I opened my eyes in my old room. One thing I hated was being tied up, too many bad memories came with that. Lenore really was a jealous bitch, she stripped it down to the walls, even my bed was gone. It didn't even feel like my house anymore, growing up it always smelled like flowers or potpourri or some scented oil. Now the whole house smelled like Sulfur Eight and perm.

"You woke, sexy?" Tony crept in the room with me. The room didn't have a lamp nor an overhead light, leaving the evening dusk to cast an eerie shadow across the one place that I used to always feel safe.

Maybe I should pretend like I'm asleep. Naw, I need to be awake if he try something. "Why are you doing this to me, Tony? I know you don't love me, but damn, I thought you at least cared a little."

"I tole you, baby," he rubbed my hair back off my face before dragging his thick tongue across the length of my face. "That pussy is magnificent. Daddy need one more baby from his baby before my mama get what's rightfully hers. Maybe me an' you can…" he murmured in my ear just as a loud crash came from downstairs. "Hmph, yo' nigga must be here to rescue you, huh. I'll go get rid of him."

I hated that ugly grin of his, but it gave me a chance to try and wiggle loose from the rope wrapped tightly around my wrists. The more I moved, it seemed like the tighter the rope became. My shoulders and wrists were on fire when the tears started to fall; I gave up. Whatever Daddy left me, Lenore could have. I lived my life fine without it all these years, fuck it. I wasn't a superhero. If it would get me untied I was all in.

I heard something downstairs that started as tussling and turned into an all-out brawl. "Who the…no don't shoot him! Don't shoot him!" Lenore screamed before three loud pops echoed through the house. *Déja vu like a muthafucka.*

Footsteps stormed up the steps and in the room to where I rocked back and forth, eyes squeezed shut. I didn't want to see the people who would ultimately be responsible for my death, my only prayer was that they made it quick… "Cary?"

"Do it and get it over with! If it's time for me to be with my parents…wait, what…what are you doing?"

"Juelz and Leonidas waiting on you." The Creole-looking Arab man untied me as he spoke. "Come on get in the car, we'll make sure you get home aight."

"Wait, so you aren't…"

"Time for me to move back to the Chi, I'm convinced all this sun got y'all muthafuckas crazy," he uttered, escorting me down the steps. Tony's dead body laid in the middle of the floor with his eyes still open, a permanent scowl etched across his features. Lenore was on the couch snoring, her lip still swollen in the spot where I hit her and a purple bruise forming slowly on her right cheek. "Your stepmother gonna wake up with a hell of a headache, but I'm gonna leave her life up to you. Stay safe, aight?" He headed to a black Wraith and climbed in as his people escorted me to a waiting Range Rover.

"Aye, who…who are you?"

"They call me God," he shot me a smile and if I wasn't already with Leonidas, I'd try and shoot my shot. "You can call me Atif."

"Atif? How do I…"

"I'll be around." He hit the push button start and hit the gas, doing sixty MPH on a residential street. Yea, I definitely been gone too long.

‡

I stood on Aunt Judy's porch adjusting my clothes, hoping I didn't look like Atif had been on my mind the entire time as we rode back to the city. But I did have a few questions for the man who swore I was his 'queen'. Why didn't Leonidas come pick me up? He out here shooting at folks over me, but sent somebody else to find me? Was he really in love or was it all a show because I was Ahseir Muhammed's daughter? And why did they send French Montana's

• • •
59

big brother to come get me? Lawd hammercy, that man was GORGEOUS! Talkin' bout 'call him Atif', yet he out here saving me from death and a crazy stepmother…shiiiddd, I might have to call him the one name I didn't call nobody, not even Leonidas. Lemme stop.

"Was you gonna knock, or nah?" Leonidas snapped, snatching the front door open.

"If you saw me out here, why I gotta knock?" I pushed past him and walked inside. Damn, this nigga ain't even try an' look for me, much less come get me. Ain't no way he ain't figure out where I was, now that I think about it, it was obvious. Hell, Atif found me and I didn't even know who he was. Leonidas could come get me from Meridian, Mississippi, but he had no clue of where I was in his own city. Yea, aight.

"You ok?" he swept me up into a bear hug from behind with a light squeeze.

Wiggling out of his grasp, I ran a hand through my hair to shake the last remaining thoughts of HIM from my mind. "I'm fine."

His phone buzzed on his hip and I went to the kitchen to get something to drink while he checked to see who it was. "Cary, Yenni said pull up."

I just got back, and instead of him cussing Yenni out because he was worried sick, he telling me Yenni said pull up. Leonidas acting funny all of a sudden and I ain't have time. "Aight. Lemme get the keys to your car."

"My car?"

"Don't you got a car in the garage?" I huffed, becoming more and more irritated.

"I mean, yea, but…"
"Fuck it, Leonidas. I'll call Auntie and see…"

"Cary, what they do to you?" he spun me around and gripped my shoulders.

"You said you loved me, Leonidas! You said it's always been about me!" I snapped.

"Cary, I do…"

"BULLSHIT! You love me, yet you send somebody named God to come get me?"

"Baby, I didn't…"

"And now it's 'Yenni said pull up'?" YENNI SAID PULL UP, LEONIDAS! I just got back and you telling me Yenni said pull up? What the fuck is wrong with you…"

"YOU, CARY! YOU WHAT THE FUCK IS WRONG WITH ME!" he clapped back. "How am I supposed to protect you when muthafuckas snatchin' you out the fucking crib!

"Oh, now it's my fault for getting snatched…"

"Right in front of my face! You know how the fuck I felt knowing you was out there and it wasn't a damn thing I could do about it! They call me the king of fuckin' Miami, but I had to call a nigga named God to come get you? How the fuck that look!" he raged.

"You know what? I don't know how it looks." I slid the phone from his hands and headed towards the front door. "I'll tell you what I do know though, Leonidas." I griped, snatched his keys from the end table on my way out. "Yenni said pull the fuck up. And since Lenore took my phone, I'ma snatch yours! Pull ya fuckin' skirt down, Leonidas, ya thong is showing!"

"Cary, I'ma beat yo' muthafuckin'…"

"See, THAT'S the energy you shoulda had at the house, not calling the next nigga to come do your job as my man!" I snapped. "Get'cho fuckin' life, KING!" I sneered, strolling through the front door like the house was mine.

Tapping the push button start on his key fob, I unlocked the doors and lowered myself into his Mercedes-Benz before I hit Yenni back to find out where I was pulling up to. I didn't get a head hug, a kiss, a 'you ok', didn't check me for scars…nothing but a dry ass hug. I tell this nigga don't let Lenore get away with this, yet Tony was dead from another man's hands and Lenore was somewhere still pulling air into her lungs. Now I'm seeing how much Juelz actually passed down to his kid, that stupidity gene. Hmph. Yenni said pull up, so fuck Leonidas.

Atif

Ahseir's daughter was a baddie. Even though I didn't know him personally, I still wasn't gonna disrespect the man, but this girl looked even more like Atif Jr.'s mother than Royalty did. Under normal circumstances I would've took her home, but knowing me she might've got fucked on the way. Yea, as a married man that loved my wife, I had to have the goons drive her back to the spot.

"Love, is that you?" Royalty called out from the kitchen. She had the whole house smelling like dinner and I was hungry than a muthafucka.

"Yea baby, it's me."

She met me in the doorway and gave me a big hug. "I missed you."

"Hmph, that's nice."

"Atif."

"Yea."

"Can we talk about this?"

"Bring my food upstairs." I walked briskly down the hall, not in the mood to talk to her about nothing.

"The boys called earlier," she called out behind me. "Wanted to let you know they're having fun in—"

I slammed the door before she finished. The fact that she mentioned my boys knowing what she did had my blood boiling, but truthfully it wasn't all her fault. In addition to the small shrine in my house dedicated to my second wife, I also stepped outside of my marriage. ONCE. Royalty found out and thought she was gonna do the same thing. Only thing that saved her was the fact that we had a kid together too, otherwise I woulda' buried her ass at sea. I agreed to go to counseling, but seeing that girl Cary today had me rethinking some things…

Leonidas

As if I wasn't already fucked up from the fact that we had to send somebody else to do what I shoulda been doing, now Cary mad at me. God claimed he wasn't gonna do nothing to her, but something happened. How we go from laying up making plans to have a baby this morning to this woman not able to stand the sight of me?

The house phone rang in the kitchen and normally I wouldn't disrespect my parents by answering their phone, but Cary just took mine so it might be important. "Yea."

"That's how you answer the phone at my house?" Ma huffed in my ear. "'Yea?' What if I was somebody who had some important news?"

"If that was the case, you woulda' called one of the twins," I replied. Ma swore she had one up on me, but I loved her regardless. "What's the word?"

"Nothing. Just wanted to see how things were going back home," she spoke wistfully. "I miss Miami."

"Ain't nothing changed, still same ol' bullshit with the same ass people," I huffed, peeking out the window to see if Cary pulled back up, knowing she hadn't.

"LEONIDAS!"

"What, Ma?"

● ● ●
66

"I know you not cussing with me on the phone!"

"Aye, I ain't mean no disrespect, I'm just sayin'," I started pacing the bamboo floors. Yenni said pull up, but she didn't say where to. Now my mind was stuck on what they had going on. "We ain't doin' shit."

"I'm about to get off this phone before I have to cuss out my only son," she snapped. "Tell Juelz—"

"Pop said he miss you, is it cool for me to give him your number?"

"Is Lenore dead?"

"Nah."

"Tell your father he can call me when she is, then. Goodbye Leonidas." I almost heard the smirk in her voice when she ended the call.

Cary gone, Ma gone, Pop gone. These muthafuckas really left me in a ten million dollar mansion by myself with no phone and shit to do. I had to strategize on how I was gonna make this shit right with my girl so we can go off and have the happily ever after life we was meant to have. I had to fix this, but damn if I had no idea on where to start. It was gonna be a long fuckin' night.

Chapter 7

Cary

"Cary, Leonidas ain't do that," Yenni cackled as I told her the story about my little kidnapping episode. "That man truly loves you."

"I can't tell." I took another slurp of the dirty martini in front of me on the bar and watched the stripper currently on the stage. She had that booty meat fluttering back and forth like butterfly wings, sis was definitely trying to get that bag up. "Any man who loves a woman will go through hell and high water for her. My daddy told me that. Hell and high water ain't a bitch kidnapping me? In his city at that? Then he sends somebody else to come get me?"

"Girl, that's that bullshit right there," she giggled, sipping on a bottle of water. "Who came to get you, Duval?"

"Oh, so I didn't finish telling you the story." I scooted closer so I wasn't yelling over the loud music pumping through the club. "You know somebody named God?"

"Other than the Messiah himself?" Yenni giggled. "Naw."

"When I tell you this man was…" I stopped to fan myself as the images of him ran through my mental. "I can't describe him. What I can say is that I will gladly have all of his babies. And if he already got some, they can call me SM."

"SM?"

"Stepmama, bitch!" I yelled and Yenni bussed out laughing. "You know all about that life, Bash got 'bout sixty-three kids and that's only in the projects!"

"No, he only has three," she snickered, taking another swig from the bottle. "And I've met all of them, so they already know."

"For real though, Leonidas trying to make it seem like I don't have a right to be pissed, but—" I stopped when his phone started vibrating against my leg for the tenth time. There was a number that kept blowing up his text messages, but since he had facial recognition on his phone I couldn't see who it was. "This the shit I'm talking about. Ain't no niggas blowing up his phone like that and you haven't got a phone call! Yenni call this number back for me."

We got up and walked outside so I could hear who answered the phone. "What is it?"

"305-579-6111."

It rang twice before I heard the call connect. "Who the fuck is this?"

"Bitch, who the fuck are you?" Yenni snapped before I could stop her.

"You know who you called! And yes, me and that nigga bout to fuck right now!" She cackled that hoe laugh and I knew exactly who it was. I snatched the phone from her hand and hung up before I blocked the number.

"Cary, who—"

"So, this nigga still got Okeema calling him after everything we went through with her and her nasty aunt," I was so pissed I had to stop myself from shaking. "Like really, nigga? Is the pussy that fuckin' good? What's your excuse for him now, Yenni?"

"You right sis. Usually I'd try and defend him, but it ain't no coming back from this one," she shook her head and stared down the street. "I mean, y'all kidnapped this hoe a few weeks ago, she escapes, her aunt pops up at yo' house—"

"Crazy thing is, that's not her aunt," I interrupted. "That's that bitch mama! I know it, but I don't even know if he knows it! So now you basically fucking my stepsister! And I'm thinking about this the whole time I'm riding back from my old house to his mama house...like how could he NOT know, considering Juelz passed the game down to him?"

"Yea...yea, you right, sis. You right." Yenni agreed.

"My thing is: now I find out you and this girl still got a connection," I continued. "You and this girl still talking. You and this girl still communicating, like you wasn't there when Benny stuck that needle in her arm and tossed her in the trunk of his car. Nine times outta ten, if this girl still calling you this time of night,

● ● ●
70

blowing your phone up back to back, you and this girl still fucking. Am I right, Yenni?"

"We don't know that though, Cary. He could just be trying to get information from—"

"FUCK INFORMATION!" I kicked a garbage can as we walked down the street trying to cool myself off. "What type of information he getting this time of night, Yenni? So if it was you and somebody snatched you up off the street, somebody you DON'T KNOW come and give you the protection you should've got from Bash, then you find out he was laid up with one of his pieces while you was out there praying whether you lived or died, would you be saying 'oh, he was trying to get information'? Would you be cool with Bash moving like that?"

"Hell the fuck naw!" she snapped, slamming her water bottle against the concrete. "I'd be bashing that nigga's skull in!"

"My point exactly! Two weeks, Yenni? You had two weeks to cut off all communication with this girl and didn't, yet I'm supposed to be the rational one? Not today, Satan! Not to-fucking-day!"

As we were on the sidewalk going back and forth, a gunmetal gray Range Rover with tinted windows pulled up and parked but nobody got out. I noticed it when the truck parked, but once I realized whoever was still inside, I nudged Yenni, knowing she kept a pistol on her regardless of her condition. "Yenni, I know you see these muthafuckas at this curb, right?"

"I been saw them. Don't trip sis, I guarantee my trigger finger ain't nothing to play with," she spoke calmly. "Pregnant or not, they gonna have to kill me first."

"I shouldn't have never—" I began, but stopped when the driver's side door opened and shut. Now I understood why he had the name he did, because this man was truly everywhere I turned. "Shit Yenni, that's him," I whispered loudly.

"Who?"

"God."

"Cary, what makes you think God driving when he can just…oh my God," she stopped when he rounded the front of the truck with a panty-soaking smile. "Girl, fuck King. He still talking to Okeema anyway," she whispered back.

"That's all I'm saying." I flicked my head slightly so I could run my fingers through my hair real quick without looking too thirsty. "So. We meet again." I cheesed all in this grown man's face. Yea, Leonidas was an adult, but God was GROWN. There was a big difference between the two.

"I thought that was you out here yelling and cussing. What's a woman with a mouth as beautiful as yours doing talking like that?" he flirted back.

"Uhmm…"

"She just found out some fucked up…" Yenni stopped to clear her throat, "…messed up news. Cary was just venting, right sis?"

"Yea," I stumbled as Yenni nudged my rib cage so hard I almost hit the wall. "Crazy."

"Hmm." He stroked his beard while his eyes roamed across my frame. "Didn't we just drop you off a while ago?"

"Yea, but I needed some space."

"Space, huh." God looked back and forth between me and Yenni before his eyes landed on me again. "I guess you would need some space when yo' nigga got an overinflated ego that has no room for anyone else but himself, even after his queen was kidnapped. But that's a conversation for another time. Enjoy your night, love."

God gave me one last look before he headed towards the entrance to the strip club as I exhaled. I didn't realize I was holding my breath until I let it go while Yenni watched him walk away. "That's God? That's the man who came and got you?"

"Yea."

"Like I said before, fuck King." Yenni repeated for a second time. "If he out here playing 'pick me' games with you and Okeema, tag you in a God," she snickered.

"You think so?"

"That man just got you pregnant with his eyes, shit I know so!" she giggled. "You got his number?"

"Naw, but I should have, right?" I licked my lips at the thought of what this man could do to me behind closed doors and damn near followed him back inside, but again, I didn't want to look thirsty.

"If you haven't heard nothing I said tonight, hear this: fuck King. Go be somebody's stepmama," Yenni snorted. "That man is fucking gorgeous!"

"Lemme get Leonidas's car back before he send Benny out here...wait," I squinted at the back Impala with the black matte rims creeping down the street. "This nigga swear he ain't obvious!"

Yenni turned to see what I was looking at and saw Benny's car park across the street. "What's up, nigga! You so fuckin' aggy, let King send you out here to babysit Cary!"

"I ain't sent nobody nowhere!" Leonidas yelled out the driver's side window before he climbed out the car. "Cary—"

I walked over and met him halfway in the middle of the street, fuming. Seeing Atif calmed me down for a few minutes, but laying eyes on this man for a second time had my blood boiling all over again. I refused to act up in public for a second time that night, God was right. "Here's your keys, here's your phone. Thank you for letting me use it, but I'll get another one tomorrow."

"What?"

"Listen, we tried out the lil' date thing, it worked for a hot second, now it's not," I continued. "What we gonna do. Let's not make this hard, aight?"

"Cary, what you talking about?" For some reason he was confused, so I pointed to his phone to help him out.

"Oh, your lil' hoe been calling you all night," I spoke sweetly, flipping the phone face up so he could see the missed notifications. "I think she trying to get some dick, you should call her back."

"My what?" His eyes slid downward to check the number and he knew he was busted. "Cary, I can explain—"

"I'm good, love. Yenni, can you drop me off at the hotel? I'm tired."

"Yea, I'll drop you off," Yenni smirked while Leonidas stood in the middle of the street stuck. "Where we going?"

"I got a standing reservation at the Versacé mansion," I yawned, purposely switching my ass so Leonidas could see what he was giving up to fuck with a known bust down. "Guess I'll start looking for another house tomorrow."

"Cary, you know you can come stay with me—" Leonidas called himself trying to be chivalrous, not knowing it was too late for that shit.

"No thank you." I waved one more time before I lowered myself down into Yenni's car. It was time for me to live the life I wanted, not what everybody else told me I should be living. Yea, Leonidas was the king of Miami, but that didn't necessarily mean I was his queen.

Chapter 8

Leonidas

"The fuck was that all about?" I questioned aloud. Me and Benny pulled up on this damn girl to talk some sense into her and she spending the night at the Versacé mansion? I had his car because he could vouch for me about that nigga God, Benny knew as well as I did that Pop gave that order, not me. Cary wasn't trying to hear nothing I had to say and it was some bullshit.

"Aye, I'm bout to go in here and see some ass, since we up here at the strip club," Benny quipped. I didn't understand what the allure was of women watching other women pop pussy on the stage, but every time Yenni or Cary got mad, this was where we found them. "You coming?"

I pulled out my phone and started scrolling, looking for Yenni's number. "Nah, I'm 'bout to find out—"

"Bro, you looking like you gone off the pussy right now," Benny snickered, walking towards the entrance as I admired the clean Range Rover parked in the handicapped parking spot. "She gone. If she come back, cool. If she stay gone, cool. You the king of Miami."

Shit, goddamn right I WAS the king of Miami. Like she said, Cary was my baby for a minute, but from the looks of it, now she wasn't. "Let's go watch these strippers bust that pussy open for a while. I'm tryna fuck something tonight."

We stepped in the club and dapped our people up as we moved through. Phil, the club owner that Pop knew from back in the day, came to show some love soon as we made it to the bar. "King. Didn't know you'd be in here tonight. You and Benny need a spot at the stage?"

"Nah, we'll take the usual, back in VIP."

"Ah." He looked back and forth between us and the VIP rooms.

"Something wrong?" I questioned with a pitched eyebrow.

"No, no everything's fine. I just know how you are when it comes to sharing a room and we're at capacity already."

"Aye, fuck capacity, we in here!" Benny snapped. "The fuck we look like sharing VIP with some fucking tourists!"

"Tell Becky an' nem the ballers in the building," I raised my voice so everybody, including whoever was occupying my spot, could hear me. "They can come see some real pussy another time!"

"It's not that simple," Phil continued, staring at the VIP spot. "Becky…"

God came walking out of my personal VIP with an arrogant smirk, staring at me before he kissed his teeth and addressed Phil directly. "You have some beautiful women working here, I see why the place is always packed." We got into a staring match, neither of us wanting to be the one to look away first. "I'll give you a call tomorrow to talk about the particulars. Have a good evening." Nodding in my direction, he grabbed his keys and headed towards the door. "Leonidas."

I knew this nigga's parents didn't name him what people called him, and until I found out what they did, I wasn't calling his ass God. "You too, bruh."

"King you can—" Phil started.

"Nah, I'm out. I ain't bout to be running up behind the next man like I ain't the king," I grumbled, slapping an ashtray off of the table next to me. "That ain't how this shit go!"

"Now you letting him get under your skin," Benny chuckled from behind me. "Cary ain't going nowhere for real, chill and have some fun. You need it. Hell, I need it, fucking around with Mya's ass."

"Oh, she finally started showing her true colors, huh?" I cackled on my way to the front of the club. Fuck it, we could be some regular niggas tonight.

"Man...y'all keep calling that girl crazy, and I don't see it." We sat down and signaled for one of the waitresses to come get our drink order. "Misunderstood, yeah. Crazy, ehhh..."

"All I know is, she used to go from cool to cuckoo in two point five." I watched the ass on the lil' waitress with the fat pussy as Benny told her what we wanted. "Aye, bring us some ice, too. Not the shit y'all drop on the floor and bring to niggas, make sure we get the good shit."

"I got'chu, King," she winked. Cary wanted to play games, talking 'bout me and Okeema, she needed to be worried about who I was gonna get to suck my dick tonight. "Anything else?"

"Yea, gimme yo' address so I can come through," I uttered in her ear.

"I'll text you," she mouthed back before she went to put our order in.

Benny seemed fascinated with the stripper currently twirling upside down, flipping every time she hit a full spin and still twerking each individual cheek. "Now that's talent. King, you see—"

"Wonder what Okeema wanted," I thought I grumbled to myself as I texted her back, but obviously Benny heard me.

"Aye, why you still fucking with her anyway? Thought you an' sis was trying to work on building something."

"Yea, me too, but you see how that worked out. Plus Keema got some good pussy. Now even though that ain't her fault, the girl still offering, so fuck it. Might as well, right?" I snickered. For what it was worth, I was glad we were still in contact because Cary wasn't giving me none no more, not after that shit she pulled outside.

The bottle girl came back with our drinks right on time, clinking the ice in each glass as she set them both down on the table. "King, it ain't my place to comment on what you do, but—" Benny started.

"Then don't." I tossed back the double shot of D'usse X.O. and slammed the shot glass on the table so she knew to pour me some more liquor. "I know what's best for me."

Benny looked back and forth between me and the bottle girl before he turned his eyes back to the stage. "Say less."

We watched for a while as the dancers gave us a show. Everybody in Miami knew who I was, so we didn't expect anything less. After she finished her shift, I took the bottle girl to a $40 hotel and got my dick sucked. Cary wanted to play games, what she didn't know was that I was the master at that shit.

‡

"What did you want last night, Okeema?" I just stepped out the shower when this hoe decided to call me back. Low key, it was her fault that I wasn't laid up in my favorite pussy, so whatever she wanted was gonna have to wait.

"You told me to call you after I got home. I thought you was coming this way," she whined.

"What did we talk about before that?"

"King I'm tired of going back and forth with you over this hoe!" she snapped. "Every time I turn around, it's 'where's Lenore, where you think she at', all that other shit! I told you I don't know! And if I did know, why would I tell you when you act like we ain't—"

"Keema, listen to me," I took a deep breath in and blew it out so I didn't cuss this girl out. "You fucked my father. In my mama house. Then came in the room and fucked me. What makes you think things just gonna go back to what they were—"

"Right!" she interrupted, trying to get her point across. "We still fucked after that! Which is why I don't see why now all of a sudden it's a problem—"

I hung up on her ass. This girl was stupider than I thought she was and I was two seconds off of cussing myself out for texting her in the first place. Cary always talking about what I wasn't doing, but I was out here trying to get Lenore tied up in a cage once and for all. Had she listened to me from the get-go, we wouldn't be having these problems.

I told her to put a bullet in that woman's head when we first caught her slipping, but nah, she wanted to plot and plan on how she wanted to torture this bitch. Now she out here loose again and doing her own kidnapping schemes. I'm convinced they actually got love each other for real and don't want to admit it, because both of them let the other one get away.

Okeema rang my phone for a second time and I put her on do not disturb. Her dumb ass was disturbing the fuck outta my peace while I was trying to get my head together. Benny was right, Cary had me out here looking like one of those in-love niggas when that wasn't who I was for real. I was the king of Miami. Pussy fell in my lap on a regular, along with some other things.

Duval was hitting my line next and I picked up for my hitta in command. "Yea."

"Aye, you know Phil selling the strip club?"

"So? What that gotta do with me?"

"I just got off the phone with Benny and he was telling me you got heat with somebody named God?"

The mere mention of his name had my blood boiling all over again, but he didn't need to know that. "I ain't got no issues with that man."

"King. This me, bruh. If you got problems—"

"Why the fuck you and Benny so pressed about what I got going on!" I roared. These niggas was beginning to piss me off. "I said I ain't got no issues with that man! Y'all actin' like some lil' hoes, straight up!"

"Aye, I see you got some other shit going on, so let me let you go. Oh yea, by the way, tell Cary Tianna been trying to get in contact with her, something about a girl's trip or something she said. I'll get up with you later, King."

He rushed off the phone before I told him don't be delivering no fuckin' messages to me about Cary. I tossed the phone on the bed and went back to getting dressed. "Fuck her."

Chapter 9

Cary

I can get used to this.

I woke up in the middle of the double queen sized bed and stretched my arms towards the painted ceiling in the Signature Suite at The Villa Casa Casuarina, formerly Gianni Versacé's mansion. Even though I left my money at the old house, I still wasn't broke, so there was no sense in me living like I didn't have it like that. Queens didn't walk around heartbroken, if the king wanted to act up, we replaced his ass. Since the streets of Miami was asking about a queen, I'ma flip my hair and look back while I'm twerking in the mirror.

After taking care of my hygiene, I got dressed and walked outside to wait for my Uber Black to pull up. The same gunmetal gray Range Rover from last night hopped in front of a black Escalade and the driver rolled down the passenger side window. "They say when you run into somebody three times in twenty-four hours, you supposed to let them take you out for breakfast," Atif's voice came from inside. "You hungry?"

"Sure." I cancelled the request for a ride and hit ok when Uber said they were still charging me because my driver was already at the pick-up spot. "Where we going?"

"Where you wanna go?" His eyes held that same twinkle from last night as he put the truck in drive and we pulled away from the curb.

"I don't know, I rarely come to this part of Miami Beach." I sat back in the comfy leather seats, watching as he waved a hand at the ceiling and the sunroof rolled backwards. "Where would you suggest?"

"Truthfully?"

"Are we gonna start our friendship off by lying to one another?" I smiled politely.

"I'd love to take you to this spot I know in Madagascar." He tapped a button on the console and I got the best massage I've ever had in my entire life from the passenger seat. "Fresh fruit, all natural ingredients. Some of the nicest people you'd ever meet. Have you been?"

"Mmm...no." I closed my eyes, rolling my shoulders backwards to get the full experience.

"Wanna go?"

"Yes...yes...yeeesss," I moaned to the truck's best feature. After yesterday happened, I needed this.

"So that's what it sounds like when that lil' pussy cum, hmm..." Atif leaned over while we were at a stop light to whisper in my ear. "Noted."

"Huh? Oh…I'm…I'm so sorry," I sat up, embarrassed. He wasn't supposed to hear that.

"Oh, don't be sorry, baby. We gotta keep something between ourselves, right?" he winked as the light turned green. "Like I was saying though, can I take you to where I wanna go? I don't wanna cause no friction in a happy home unless it ain't happy."

"But I'm hungry now. How long is it gonna take for us to get there?"

"You right," he agreed. "I know a nice Cuban spot not too far from here, but it's good to know you would've been up for going out the country with me."

"Cuban sounds good," I blushed. Atif was doing things to me… "Do you mind if we make a quick pit stop? I gotta pick up a new phone."

"Sure."

I laid my head back on the seat and watched the city glide by. King couldn't be mad at me because truth be told, it was his fault Atif and I met in the first place. Had he followed Lenore like I told him to and grabbed her on the steps, we wouldn't be in this situation; she had the keys to the van. Realizing the truck stopped, I looked around and noticed we pulled up to the AT&T store in no time. "Uhmm…I have T-Mobile."

"That's nice." Atif smirked before he got out and rounded the truck to open my door.

"We at the AT&T store though."

"Leonidas gonna get mad if he knows I paid for you a new phone?" he smiled, escorting me inside.

"Naw, I'm just…never mind." Whether he would be mad or not wasn't my concern. He wasn't the one making sure I was able to communicate, so fuck 'em.

Atif bought me the same phone he had and took me to the Apple store to get my name engraved on the back. After that, we spent the day together. We grabbed something to eat before he took me shopping, then we went for a long walk on the pier and just got to know each other better. He told me about his second wife that he was in love with who passed away while giving birth to his first son, and how he stepped up to take care of her little brothers. He also told me about his third wife who he thought was the one, but she cheated on him. Unlike most men, he blamed himself in a way, since he cheated first he felt she only did so to teach him a lesson.

Even I knew you don't cheat on a man like Atif, there was something about his overall presence that screamed boss. Leonidas had it too, but on Atif it was more masculine, more primal, more…I don't know. What I did know was that the more he talked, the more I wanted him in the worse way.

● ● ●

Atif's lips were moving, but I hadn't heard a word he said. "Huh?"

"I said what about you?" he smiled warmly. "I hear a lot about your father on the streets, but that doesn't tell me what kind of man he was."

"He was a lot like you, to be honest," I spoke, my head filled with fond memories of life with my daddy. "People respected and feared him, but he was an honorable man."

"Is that how you see me?"

"From our conversation, yea."

"Hmm." Atif stroked his beard, seemingly lost in thought. "I don't think anyone has ever used the word 'honorable' when describing me. Deadly, yea. Killer, hell yea. Honorable…now that you mention it, I guess I am."

"Can I ask you a question?"

"Ask away."

I paused for a second to lose myself in his hazel-gray orbs, this man was dangerous and I wasn't talking about the streets. A married man who was scorned…men don't show their emotions like women do, but that doesn't mean they don't have any. "Are you happy?"

"Am I happy." He turned his gaze away from me to look out over the ocean's waves. "I used to be, but lately I can't say I know what that is anymore."

"Why not?"

"Don't get me wrong, I know what happy is. I felt that with my second wife, and in the beginning, with my third wife too. Nowadays, I'm feeling like I don't know how to live. At least not like I used to. At this point I'm taking it day by day." He spoke truthfully.

"Everyone should know what it feels like to be happily married," I spoke up. "Do you think that you might be going through a rough patch with your wife? Not all marriages are sunshine and rainbows all the time, it's gonna rain eventually."

"And I get that. At first I wondered if it was just me. I've seen a lot of death, and not just from the streets. Losing friends, losing the people I love, the people that were important to me...I closed myself off from a lot. That's why when Royalty cheated, I wondered if I was a part of that. But if you see your spouse going through something, ain't that when you supposed to come closer together? I just felt like there were times when she knew I was hurting and didn't give a fuck."

"But you said you cheated first."

"I did, but I owned up to my bullshit early," he revealed. "When it happened, I felt guilty like a muthafucka. Told the lil' bitch she couldn't suck my dick no more and blocked her number, then came home and admitted what I did that same night. Asked her to forgive me, and she goes out a week later and does the same shit? A week? You can't tell me she didn't already know that man! On top of that, she did more than let another man taste her, she actually went out and fucked him! Then tried to hide it like they don't call me God. That's the shit I'm talking about!"

The same way he felt about his wife cheating on him was the same way I felt last night when I found out Okeema was still calling Leonidas's phone. In all honesty, we probably could've got past the whole him not coming to get me thing in a few days after I calmed down and thought about it. But there was no coming back from him still contacting a bitch who was an enemy to me knowing she was a part of the scheme to have me killed. "I know exactly what you mean."

"I don't involve myself in the next man's business, and right now I'm probably feeling a little vulnerable, so is there anywhere I can drop you off?" Atif was a true gentleman, regardless of what his reputation was on the street.

"I'm staying at the hotel where you picked me up for now, so you can drop me back off out there."

We rode back to the room in silence, both consumed with our own thoughts. I didn't know what he was thinking, but I was wondering why this man had such bad luck with women. Then again too, his second wife's passing wasn't his fault. That wasn't anybody's fault. Hell, who was I to talk, before I got back to Miami my life was pretty fucked up too. They say everyone has a twin flame, that one person who the universe destined to be together. Sometimes we found that person, sometimes we spent our lives never coming in contact with the person who held the second part of our soul. And sometimes we were blessed with two.

I started getting myself together a few blocks from the hotel, reaching for my bags that he threw in the back seat after we left the mall. "Need me to walk you inside?"

"I got it," I wheezed, trying to grab the last bag that seemed determined to stay out of my reach. "You've already done too much, putting me on your plan and taking me shopping."

"It's no big deal. Just wanted to show my appreciation for you allowing me to vent, that's all." He pulled up to the valet desk and motioned for someone to assist. "Plus what kind of man would I be if I didn't make sure you got upstairs safe? This hotel is decent, but still. You never know who out here lurking in the hallways pretending like they work here."

Considering I was just kidnapped the day before, thinking that the knock on my door was the maintenance man, Atif was absolutely correct. "Ok."

Grabbing my bags, he escorted me to the top floor of the hotel and to my corner suite. Once we got in, he put the bags on the couch and checked the room to make sure no one was hiding out, especially after I told him about Lenore being in my house twice. "Coast is clear, everything seems to be in order."

"Thanks again, Atif I really appreciate it." I beamed at the extra attention he showed to make sure I was good.

"No thanks needed. I'd hate to see you on the news tomorrow knowing I could've checked your suite before I left and didn't," he spoke sincerely. "Have you always had that dimple in your chin, though?"

"Huh?"

"I just noticed that dimple," he moved closer, closing the space between us to inspect my face. Palming his huge hand against my cheek, he stroked my chin ever so softly with his thumb. "Right here."

"Yea, that's always been there," I whispered, closing my eyes I leaned into his touch. "You just now noticing it?"

"Mmhmm…" The rumble in his throat had me moist for some odd reason as I laid my head on his chest through no fault of my own. My body was on auto-pilot around him and that…that couldn't happen. My feelings for this man who I just met were too strong, I couldn't…

"Cary."

"Atif…we shouldn't…" I breathed into his chest.

"We not doin' nothin'," he mumbled, running his fingers through my hair. "Two friends looking out for each other, right?"

"Right."

"Your hair smells good," he spoke from above my head. "Coconut oil?"

"Marula and rosemary." The more he spoke, the more I lost myself in his strength. "Your shirt soft. Cotton?"

"Silk and cotton blend. Feels good on that chocolate skin, don't it?" he murmured in my ear.

"Mmhmm…"

"Did you enjoy yourself today?" he questioned gently.

I felt his fingertips graze my back slowly…up and down with the faintest stroke. "Yes, thank you."

Atif leaned down and nestled his face in the crook of my neck, sniffing my skin. "Good. Can I tell you a secret?"

"Yes."

"I dreamt about you last night," he whispered in my ear.

Crazy...because I dreamt about him too. "Did you?"

"Mmhmm. Wanna know what you was doing?"

Something told me don't ask, but..."What?"

"Standing in the middle of my bed dressed in some white lace boy shorts with no bra...oouu wee." His hand moved to the back of my neck with his thumb delicately stroking one of my pressure points. "Begged me to let you put your ankles on my shoulders..."

"And what you do?"

"Laid you down, licked you from your neck to your waist, and peeled those panties off with my teeth," he breathed, his third leg poking me from the front. "Slipped my hand between your thighs and played with that pussy like this." His hand slipped down the front of my shorts and I felt his thumb slowly pulsate against my nub. "Why you so wet? I was just telling you about my dream."

"Why you so hard?" I murmured against his ear. "My pussy always wet."

"Wet is one thing, this lil' pussy got a tsunami goin' on." He slipped two fingers in and out of me slowly as my breath pitched and retreated. "Do you like the fact that I woke up with you on my mind and had to go let one off so I didn't call my wife your name?"

● ● ●

I didn't know what this man was doing to me, but I did know I didn't want it to end…ever. "Atif—"

"I'ma give you a choice tonight. Wanna know what that is?"

"Mmhmm…" I whined lowly, Atif was pushing me closer and closer to the edge. I didn't want to fall off the cliff, but…

"You want oral or anal?"

"Oh God!" My legs went weak, Atif caught me as I bit my lip, trying not to scream while my orgasm poured from between my thighs as he manipulated my little bud until she opened up and showed her true beauty. "Atif—"

With one move, my feet left the floor only to be laid across the couch before Atif buried his face between my thighs. "Gimme every last drop, baby…I can take it." My body jerked erratically back and forth against his lips as I did what I was told, and took all of him in. "Mmm…how a man can let you go I don't know."

I needed that. I needed every piece of what just happened. As I ran my fingers through his curly locks debating on whether I should give him a second taste, I jumped when the knock came at the door.

"Leonidas must've sniffed the air and smelled you with another man," Atif snickered. "I'm 'bout to go wash my face, although if you want me to stay…"

The knock came again, this time a little more urgent. "Atif, I can't…"

He grabbed my face and stuck his tongue down my throat, savoring every bit of my juices. I palmed the back of his head and kissed him back like it was our wedding night and I was ready to fuck. "Cary!" Yenni's voice called out. "Sis, you aight in there?"

"Go ahead and talk to your friend. I'll get cleaned up and get out y'all hair, aight?" He planted one last peck against my lips. Gazing in his eyes, I knew there was gonna be a war coming soon.

"Yea...here...here I come." I pulled my shorts back on and limped to the door. This man hadn't put dick in me, but that hurricane tongue of his had me feeling good and fucked already. "Hey...hey, Yenni. Girl, what's...uhmm...everything ok?"

"Cary, what's wrong with you?" She crept cautiously across the threshold, eyeing me suspiciously. "You let Lupe an' them slip you summa that angel dust? You know they say...ooohh, hello. God, right?" she cheesed knowingly as Atif stepped out the bathroom.

"That's me. Aye Cary, I'll text you later, aight?" he turned on that million dollar smile as I sat on the couch blushing.

"Ok."

"Come walk me to the door. Uhmm, Yenni right? She'll be right-right back."

"Oh, don't mind me!" Yenni went to hit up the mini fridge in the bedroom.

As soon as we got to the door, he wrapped his big hands around my waist and pulled me close for the second time. "I wanna see you later," he growled lowly. "So we can finish what we started."

Should I be worried about his wife? Obviously he wasn't. "Tonight?"

"Mmhmm."

"Lemme see what I can do and I'll let you know."

"Either way, we gotta take you car shopping tomorrow so people not popping up on you," he smirked. "I'm sure she came over here to see if you needed anything, like a good friend would."

"Oh yea, I forgot to text her my new number."

"Go ahead and get caught up with yo' girl. I'll be back to check on you, aight?" he leaned down and planted another kiss on my lips.

"Ok."

Atif left and I leaned against the door to exhale, yet again. Damn, why was he married though? And why wasn't HE the one to come to Meridian, Mississippi to pick me up? Like Yenni said yesterday, fuck Leonidas.

"How was it?" Yenni snickered with her feet kicked up on my bed watching The Real Housewives of Atlanta.

"How was what?"

She smacked her lips and took a sip from the can of Pepsi she got from the mini fridge. "The dick."

"We didn't have sex."

"Hmph, y'all did something."

"What makes you think—"

"Your hair messed up, for one. For two, your jean shorts on backwards," she snickered. "Now if you didn't realize that, something else gotta be occupying your mind, sis!"

"I uhmm—"

"I just wanna know if it was good," Yenni smacked her lips again, taking another sip from the can. "You ain't never been that flustered around King, that's all I'm saying. What you do and who you do it with is your business."

"BITCH!" I plopped down on the bed next to her and got comfortable. "That man spoke whatever his native language is to my pussy the whole time! Had me laying on the couch stuck, you was knocking on the door and I couldn't even remember the words I needed to say to answer you! That's the real reason it took me so long!"

"Bitch you lying!"

"My right hand to God…wait…"

"He got a big dick though," she sighed, rolling her eyes at the TV.

"How you know?"

"That muthafucka was so long…he must've tried to tie it up with the drawstring from his jogging pants but that monster was still trying to break free," she cackled. "I could've sworn I saw the tip laid up against the top of his belly button. Cary you betta do some squats, fast, pray, something because if you and that man ever fuck he putting you in the hospital!"

"Girl me and Atif ain't—"

"Bitch you limping and you said all he did was gave you some neck, fuck you talmbout what you and that man ain't doing!" she snapped jokingly.

"Yenni."

"What."

"Me and Leonidas ain't gonna make it, are we?"

"I'ma say it one more time in case you forgot: FUCK KING. That's his fuck up and his loss."

"Atif is married though," I reasoned.

"Who is Atif?"

"God. His real name is Atif."

"Oh. Like I said, that's King's dumb ass fault. You ain't gotta marry the man, have you some fun. You don't know his wife and she don't know you. If sis call herself trying to rumble, shit call us the muthafuckin' Bey hive, because we always gonna protect the queen whether you with King or not."

"That's why I love you, bitch." I snuggled closer to Yenni and watched Ne-Ne cuss out damn near every one of her cast members like she did all the time. "I can't believe this show still comes on."

"Ratchet sells regardless." Yenni smacked on some popcorn while my mind went back to Atif spelling his name across my clit over and over before his tongue dipped inside my gooeyness. I needed something to take my mind off this man, and quick. "Aye, what you doing tomorrow?"

"Nothing, why?"

"We was supposed to go to Jacksonville to see the land my father left me, remember?"

"Oh yea. Tomorrow would be the perfect day to do that," she smacked, dropping kernels in my bed.

"Excuse you, I gotta sleep here!"

"My bad, I'll clean that up. But yea, I just gotta let Bash know—"

"Don't tell Bash. He gonna tell Leonidas and I'm not in the right headspace to deal with him."

"You right. Road trip!"

"Speaking of road trip, lemme call Tianna to see if she trying to go too."

"Ok. Aye, see if Atif got a brother, just in case this whole thing with me and Bash don't work out," she snickered.

"I got'chu sis."

Chapter 10

Leonidas

I hadn't heard from Cary nor Yenni all day. I knew she didn't have a phone, but Yenni wasn't answering her shit either. Why this girl thought it was fine for her to be moving around the city with no phone was beyond me, but Cary seemed to think she was invincible so I let her have that. She'll call when Lenore get behind her ass and she need me again.

Stepping in the deserted warehouse on the water, I hit the bodyguard standing at the door with a head nod before I headed to the back for our monthly meeting. It was too much shit going on with everybody we knew, so I called a meeting to strategize on how we was gonna fix this shit once and for all. The suppliers down in Mexico were becoming reckless again, and Pop hit me earlier talking bout I needed to go back down to Medellin. He needed to send somebody else to handle that because I wasn't going.

"Whaddup Pop." I dapped the team up on the way to my seat, grabbing a cigar from the humidor before I sat down. "What's the word?"

"You and Cary need to go down to Medellin to have a discussion with our new suppliers, just so they know we are not to be fucked with. Where is she, by the way?"

"I don't know." I grabbed my phone and responded to the text from the lil' bottle girl from last night who was trying to see me after her shift at the strip club.

"You don't know?" Pop stared at me with a raised eyebrow. "Leonidas, we had this discussion! She has a seat at this table and should be here as well!"

"Look, I ain't that girl's keeper!" I snapped. "Y'all keep telling me I'm losing her and she ain't mine to fuckin' lose! If you wanna know where she at, go find her y'all damn selves because she ain't my responsibility!" I slammed a fist down on the table.

Pop's gaze was fixated on me through my tirade, and he nodded his head slightly when I was done. "Hmm. Aight. Duval, take Bash with you and go down to Medellin. I need you to have a conversation with José Nunez. We'll get you the information later. Any new business?"

"Phil selling the strip club," Duval spoke up. "We need to be making plans to talk to the new owner, right?"

"God is the new owner. We not gonna have any problems outta him, he good."

God. AGAIN. "Aye, who is God and why he got all this clout in my city?"

Pop took another pull from his cigar and blew smoke in the air introspectively. "Me and Ahseir needed help with a situation and we had to make some phone calls. Of course we reached out to our team first, but this was something we had to go out the country to take care of. Abraham, you remember?"

"Yea." Abraham was one of the original members of their team back in the day who still showed up for meetings. His kids dabbled in the game, but for the most part he was grandfathered in, like Donnell. "That situation with the guerillas from overseas who came over here trying to infiltrate what we got going on. No matter who we sent to handle it, we got reports of our people coming up dead. Ahseir got *Karich's* number from somebody, next thing we knew those niggas were the ones dead. Nobody came and said nothing to us before or afterwards."

"With the threat eliminated, we forgot about it," Pop continued where Abraham left off. "We lived our lives. Ahseir was the only person with this man's phone number, so after he passed away we literally had no contact with him. Then, 'bout five years ago, this man pops up outta nowhere at the club and told us he was Karich's son. Told us we were indebted to them for the situation they took care of and knew intimate details about what went down."

"And you ain't do shit?"

"Like I said, these niggas literally went from strong arming our people, popping us off one by one to dead in the span of six hours. We ain't paid nobody, we ain't talked to nobody, nobody came and said 'ok, we took care of that lil' situation', nothing. Then somebody shows up outta nowhere, just like they did, still not wanting no money but said call them if something came up that we needed help with? What was I supposed to do, Leonidas? Shoot him?"

"If that's what it took!"

"Gentlemen, give us the room," Pop locked eyes with me a second time as everyone filed out of the space. "What's the problem, son? Because I'm not going up against a man with that much power without a good reason."

I checked my phone to see if I had a missed call or text from a number that wasn't saved in my phone. Cary had to call me eventually. "Ain't no problem, Pop."

"Something's going on." He rubbed his beard, still staring at me astutely. "It's Cary, ain't it?"

I picked up the cigar sitting in the ashtray about to burn out and took a long pull, letting the smoke burn my lungs for a little bit. "Pop, excuse my language, but fuck Cary."

"Mmhmm." He finally broke his gaze, checking his own phone buzzing across the table. "King, I can't tell you what to do. You gotta make your own mistakes in life, that's the only way you gonna learn. Don't think you fooling nobody but yourself when everybody see you spazzing out one minute and checking your phone every five seconds when it hasn't rung. If you love that woman, go after her.

You keep telling the world 'fuck Cary', knowing you love the fuck outta that woman."

My phone buzzed and I sent the lil' bottle girl the address to one of my trap spots on the water. These lil' bitches loved making videos of them getting fucked on the balconies like they was the main bitch, little did they know my main got that action from me on the yacht. "Pop, Cary is the last thing on my mind right now," I lied. Shit, I couldn't get her out of my fucking head.

"Don't end up like me and your mother, son," he advised. "By the way, I need that—"

"She said don't call her until Lenore is dead."

"That's it." Pop laid both hands flat on the table and pushed himself up, checking the pistol in his waistband. "Ju-Ju has spoken. Let's go kill this bitch."

"See that's a plan I can get behind right there," I followed suit. "Lemme grab Killa and Benny so we can ride the fuck out."

☦

We passed that same gunmetal gray Range Rover from last night on our way to Unc's old crib on Sunset Grove Lane going in the opposite direction. "You think she here?"

"Honestly, no. Only because she know Cary knows where she is," Pop spoke. "Lenore not gonna sit around and wait to get caught, she gonna go somewhere else and hide in plain sight until she feel like she got what she wants."

"That's fucked up."

"Then again too, she might still be here because like I said, she hides in plain sight. Could be thinking we not gonna come back out here since we knew she was here."

We parked one street over and walked back to the house. Killa and Benny circled around the back while me and Pop knocked on the front door to see if she would answer. "Don't look like nobody here." I peered through the open windows to see if anyone was inside moving around.

I got a text and stopped being nosy to check it. "Pop, Benny said come round the back, something we gotta see."

We went around to the back of the house where Benny and Killa stood over what looked like a body with a foot hanging out of the garbage can. "Aye, that's that fuck nigga that came to the house with Lenore to snatch Cary up!"

"Look like somebody else got to him before we could," Benny smirked. "Y'all talked to—"

"You ain't gotta say his name, we know who you talmbout," I frowned.

Pop leaned in for a second to inspect the garbage can further. "Just trying to see if they chopped his body up or if they tossed him in here whole."

"They chopped something." Killa called out from near the house.

"How you know?"

"Either this his hand over here in the grass, or it's two dead niggas out here." He kicked something towards us in the grass.

"God did this."

"Pop, how you know?"

"This exactly how we found the bodies of them niggas back in the day. If he didn't do it himself, he had it done."

For some reason, the gunmetal gray Range Rover flashed in my head a second time. I hadn't seen it anywhere in the city before last night and today. The fuck was this nigga on? "Pop, call him and set up a meeting. I wanna talk to him for a minute on some real shit."

"Leonidas—"

This nigga wanted my girl. Couldn't be nothing else but that. Why else would he ride out here and toss this nigga in the trash, leaving his hand purposely for me to find? He was too calculating to do some sloppy shit like that, Tony's hand laying in the grass was on purpose. Far as I was concerned, somebody needed to teach this nigga some boundaries. "We just need to have a conversation as men."

"I'll set it up."

Chapter 11

Cary

Yenni was able to watch another episode of Real Housewives before Bash started blowing her phone up, saying Juelz was sending him down to Medellin. They went back and forth on text for a second before she got mad and left. I saw that happening anyway, so it wasn't a big deal when it actually played out.

Atif wanted me to call him back, but judging from what happened earlier, I didn't trust myself around him. Technically we were both the rebound for each other's fucked up relationships and I didn't want to get caught up in real feelings for him knowing I still felt some kind of way about Leonidas. Try as I might though, I couldn't get Atif out of my head. Every time I thought about sorting through my feelings for King, Atif's hazel-gray eyes would pop up out of nowhere. My mind wandered to how our kids might look, or whether or not his kids would accept me as their stepmother. Or even the mother to their little brother or sister, it didn't matter. As long as he was in my life in some capacity—

My text ringer brought me out of my thoughts for both men. As I was picking up the phone, a FaceTime call came in at the same time. Knowing only one person had my number, I hurried and tucked underneath the covers trying to pretend like I was asleep before I hit the answer button. "Hey."

"You didn't want me to tuck you in, huh."

I did. Atif didn't know how bad I wanted him to tuck me in, keep me warm, cuddle, spoon…and blow my muthafuckin' back out until the sun came up. "You have other obligations, I already took up your whole day."

"My kids are in Armenia with my parents, so I'm good."

"What about your wife?"

"What about her?"

"Atif, I can't—"

"You keep telling me what you can't do when I'm telling you it's ok and you can." He shifted the phone to the side for a second while he stared at something or someone off to his left side. "We must not be friends no more."

"We still friends."

"Tell me what I did wrong then, so I can fix it."

That was the problem, he ain't do nothing wrong. Everything he did was right. Too right. So right my panties were already soaking wet… "Atif we just can't."

"That's your word?"

"Yup."

"Open the door and tell me to my face, then, since that's your word."

"What?"

"You want me to knock?"

I scampered out the bed and ran to the door, peeking through the peephole to his gorgeous face trying to look intimidating. Snatching the door open with just a t-shirt and panties on, I took a minute to enjoy the view. This man…*God, why did you have to make him so perfect?* "Atif, you know we can't—"

"Is that really what you want that mouth to say to me right now?" He nudged me backwards, wrapping an arm around my waist while kicking the door closed. Atif's scent enveloped me and had my body floating on a cloud of lust that I couldn't stop if I wanted to. Luckily, I didn't want to.

"One time, and that's it, ok?"

"One time for what?" he moaned in my ear. He picked me up with one arm and I instinctively wrapped my legs around his waist, my pussy smiled when she came in contact with his dick through the thin material.

"Tonight. First and last time," I breathed before he pinned me against the wall and pecked his lips against mine. Our gentle touching quickly changed to lust as he slid his tongue between my lips. Once they met, it was magic, like we should have been together.

"You sure about that?" he moaned when we came up for air, biting my bottom lip. Atif wrapped a hand around my throat and

● ● ●

gave it a gentle squeeze while he massaged my scalp from behind with his free hand.

"Mmhmm..." I stared at him, both of our eyelids low, knowing what was about to happen and fully prepared for it to go down.

"Guess I gotta show out then, since it's our first and last time, huh." He carried me in the bedroom as I rested my head on his shoulder. Yenni was right, I could tell his dick was humongous through his blue silk jogging pants. Me and Leonidas couldn't ever have sex again because this man was about to shift my organs up somewhere near my esophagus. Atif lowered my body down on the comforter first before he pulled my shirt off and stood back to admire the view.

"You can just stick the tip in, I'm ok with that," I giggled nervously. I had to be dreaming, there was no way me and Atif were about to—

"Mmpfh, mmpfh, mmpfh. Just like I imagined," he smirked sexily. "Did I tell you I got a fetish for chocolate women?" Atif stood at the foot of the bed staring at my semi-naked body

"You didn't but I could tell," I cheesed.

"How you know?" He pulled the white tee over his head and I caught a glimpse of his perfectly sculpted body, right down to the piercing in his left nipple before he dove on the bed between my legs

● ● ●

11

and put my feet on the back of his shoulders. Taking turns peck kissing the insides of both thighs, I damn near fainted when he traced a line from my kneecaps to my pussy with his tongue. "You smell so fuckin' good."

"Mmm...Atif..."

Using his fingers, he slipped the crotch of my panties to one side and replaced the material with his tongue. "Pineapples, hmm..."

"You like that?" I breathed, rotating my hips to keep up with his pace.

"I love your tropical, chocolate self, Cary," he mumbled from beneath me. "Can I have you?"

"Yes...yes...yes...AAAHHH!"

I let out a long, silent scream with my back arched as he tilted my hips to get a better angle. "She so wet...she so fuckin' wet for me, Cary. I can't have her no more after this?"

"Ooohhh...I lied. I lied, Atif. You can have her whenever you want..."

"Turn over for me."

No matter how hard I tried, I couldn't move to save my life. "I can't."

Atif lifted up and turned me over slowly, I nestled my head in the pillow and got comfortable. "You never answered my question from earlier," he perched over me with his dick tapping my booty cheek.

"Which one?"

"Oral..." I felt his lips kiss from the base of my neck, down my spine to the top of my ass, "...or anal?"

"What you wanna do?"

"Truthfully?"

"It's too early in our friendship for us to be lying to each other," I cheesed, using my line from earlier.

Atif took a fistful of my hair and wrapped it around his hand, jerking my head back slightly as he sat the tip of his dick at the opening of my ass. "I want both."

"Then get both...ssss..."

My eyelids fluttered feeling him pulsate between my booty cheeks. Instinctively, my hand went down to stroke my bud, but his was already there. I came all over his fingertips when he slid two digits inside my slippery hole, kneading a finger across my hooded clit. "Make this pussy cum for me again," he groaned in my ear. "I got your coconut cream count up to four already, we going for ten tonight."

"Ten...oh shit..." I wheezed, collapsing on the bed as he reamed me from behind.

"That's five. Give daddy five more, baby," he moaned.

Under any other circumstances, the word daddy had me triggered, but with Atif... "Five more?"

"Mmhmm. Spread your legs for me just a little bit...like that baby," he murmured. "Just like that." Atif ran a hand across my back, lightly massaging my skin with his fingertips while he continued to slide in and out of my booty. Slowly he raised me up and hugged my body against his as he sat back on his knees and finger fucked me in one hole with his dick sliding in and out of the other, biting my neck. "You got another one for me, Cary?"

"I'm...I'm...yes. Yeeesss..."

"That's my good girl." He laid me on my back before grabbing my hips and pulled my pussy up to meet his mouth, slipping his tongue back and forth against my crease before he entered my slit. "Count it off for me."

"Se...se...seeeveeennn...seven...seeevvveeennn..." I wheezed when she exploded, my body weak from this man's high sex drive.

"Mmmm...I can't get enough of you, Cary." He laid me back on the bed and glided behind me to spoon. "You got three more in you, or you ready to tap out?"

Father, I come to you in a state of lust, please sweet Jesus please give me strength. I promise I'ma start going to church. I'ma donate to the homeless. I'm even gonna volunteer at somebody's shelter. Please Lord. Please give me the strength to go three more rounds with this man. "I got three more."

On that last dip, his dick slipped in my pussy like that was where he belonged the whole time. "I knew from the moment I saw you, baby," he rasped in my ear. "From the moment I saw you, I had to have you, Cary. Mmm…I had to have you…"

"Atif, I—I wanted you too…" I wheezed with my head down, the tip of his tongue traveling unhurriedly up the back of my neck.

"We can't go backwards from here…only forward, you hear me?"

"Only forward…ooohhh…"

"Is that number eight?"

I knew my hair was nappy as hell on my head because I kept swatting wet strands out of my eyes as the sweat poured between my titties. "Yes."

"Give it to your man, baby…"

"Atifffff…" I loved the way his name vibrated on my tongue. I don't care what nobody say, prayer works.

"You ever came like this before? That lil' pussy cream like that on demand, back to back for your man?"

"No."

"Then this makes me yours then." He kissed my shoulder before I mounted him. "Right?"

I positioned that humungous snake between my thighs, adjusting to fit his girth, his shit was big as fuck. "Me and who else?" I knew I should've rode that mechanical bull in reverse, at least that way I could've braced myself against his legs. All men like to watch their dicks slide in and out of some good pussy.

"You and you," he wheezed when I started twerking my hips. "Nobody else."

"Not even your—"

Atif raised up and meshed his tongue between my titties before we met in my mouth, moaning as he shifted my hips back and forth across his thick meat. "Nobody else but you if that's what you want. I'll divorce her tomorrow." My fingers accidentally brushed against the small dumbbell in his nipple and his dick quivered against my slick walls. "Cary I'm 'bout to...FUCK!"

I felt his warm semen pour into me and my pussy instantly responded with number nine, I was way too tired to try and stop it. Collapsing on his chest for what I hoped would be the last time, I was breathing hard as I listened to his heartbeat which matched my own. "Atif."

"Hmm?"

"You said—"

"I don't do sex talk, Cary. Anything I said to you while we were in the moment, I meant. Ball is in your court, baby."

At this point in time I didn't know what I wanted. Atif was married, and Leonidas still had a small piece of my heart. "Atif, it's just sex. We can't both just get what we need and be good?"

"What if I caught feelings for you already?"

Shit, then we both fucked up because Atif had the parts of my heart Leonidas didn't. "How? We just met."

"You don't believe a man can catch feelings from first sight?"

"No."

"Then somebody fucked your head up because it's definitely possible. Did you read the text I sent you?"

"When?"

"Right before I called." He stood up still naked and walked to the other side of the room to get my phone. "Read it."

"You know what they say about a man who gets butt naked to fuck, right?" I tucked the blanket around my titties and propped up on one elbow to watch his dick swing from side to side when he walked.

"Nah, what?"

"He either love you or you got some good ass pussy."

"Shit, they might be right because with me and you, it's both," he smirked sexily, handing me the iPhone.

I checked my notifications and saw his text: *I know we just fucking around, but wanna meet my fam and have my kids? Nothing serious. Lol, no biggie* "Lol no biggie?" I snickered.

"Nah. Nothing too serious, right?" I was surprised his smile didn't get him into more trouble than he already was.

"Well let me respond then." I typed my reply and put the phone down while he reached for his. "No Atif, that's cheating."

"Cheating?"

"Yup. You can't read it until in the morning."

"Why the morning?"

"Because that's when I'm sending you home. Come take a shower with me, you owe me one more shot of coconut cream."

"Mmhmm...that's my girl," he grinned, following me to the spa bathroom to pay his debt.

Chapter 12

Leonidas

"Aye, if I'm buying the shoes, the bundles, the purses, plus paying the bills every month…shiiiiddd nobody better not be getting nan' drop of my pussy!" Bash was in the middle of the war cabin talking shit, like he did every time he got drunk.

"Same goes for these niggas out here!" Yenni shook up with Tianna and Kimbella, who had never been out here before now. "Shiiiddd, real bitches buy our own stilettos and Louie bags, check a bag while we twerk to City Girls outside that mini mansion that y'all niggas paid for! Don't get it fucked up baby, it's still a hot girl summer in the M.I.A. bitches!"

"Yenni don't make me beat yo' muthafuckin' ass in front of yo' lil' friends," he rushed over to growl in her ear. "Act like you got some sense!"

"Nah, act like you know what the fuck it is, Bash!" she snapped. "Nobody bet not be getting a drop of whose pussy? Huh? Can't hear you, pooh!"

"Here you go with that bullshit again," he tried to wave her off. "You heard what the fuck I said!"

"Yup, my nigga, I sure did! Now keep that same energy tonight when I don't come home. You of all people know what they say about pregnant pussy."

"Home?" Killa caught that last part before everybody else. "Bash, you and Yenni together or some shit?"

"Not only are they together, who you think sponsored that lil' bun in her oven?" Tianna cheered. "Everybody raise your glasses! We celebrating Santiago's return, Bash and Yenni, and—"

"Drink up, niggas." I was the first to toss back the double shot of Reposado, slamming my shot glass into the fireplace. Don't get me wrong, I was happy for Santiago, Bash, Yenni and low key Duval and Tianna. My lil' brother popped the question the other day and she accepted. The downside to that was that I hadn't laid eyes on Cary Muhammed in about two months.

Yenni still talked to her, but she was given explicit directions not to give me her contact information. I thought about following her when they were supposed to meet up, but Yenni was smarter than that. I even hired a private detective to find her who gave me my money back the next day.

When Cary handed me my phone and car keys back that night, I should've worked it out right then and there, but my pride was bruised. I was supposed to be her Superman, I was her hero after Uncle Ahseir died. I was the one she was supposed to be able to depend on. Where I fucked up was when I sent another nigga to do the job reserved for me in her eyes.

Then on top of that, I knew Okeema was still calling but I didn't care. I used to tell my woman I was out looking for Lenore when in actuality I was out getting sucked up by my ex. Cary would've done it if I asked her, but with Okeema I didn't have to ask. She knew what I liked and what I didn't like. She knew how to make it nasty and keep it that way. She knew how to soften her forehead, unclench her jaw and relax her shoulders right before she inhaled my balls. Shit, I even liked when me and the bitch argued because that made the pussy even better. Pop fucked around on Ma for years and she only found out recently. As far as I was concerned, I was a lot more cautious than he was when it came to this shit. In the end, I fucked up.

When Yenni finally broke down and told me Cary wasn't staying at the Versacé mansion anymore, my dumb ass went home to wait for her to show back up so we could talk about it. I waited for two days before I realized she wasn't coming. Then I blamed everyone around me for fucking up my relationship. I blamed Pop for keeping in contact with Lenore in the first place, I blamed Benny for not stopping me that night, I blamed Yenni for not telling me about the trip they took to Jacksonville where she decided to stay. I even blamed the nigga God for going to grab her from that little kidnapping situation.

I took a ride up I-95 to talk some sense into her, but since I didn't know anyone in the city directly, I bent a few corners and came home. Taking that five hour drive back alone, I had more than enough time to think. Being the king of Miami had its perks, but on the flip side it also had its downfalls. I could go in any club and get love off rip, niggas saluted when I hit the blocks. And the bitches would bust down simply because they chased that clout the same way they checked a bag. The downside was that all that shit would always be there, but there was only one Cary Muhammed.

Jaden came out on the porch and dapped me up before handing me another glass of liquor. "Did you find her?"

"Wherever she is, she's not using her social security number." His whole demeanor, just like the rest of the squad, was discouraged. They built a real bond with her and for her to disappear…well, for her to leave me like that…fuck it. "Yenni still talk to her, right?"

"That's the only reason I'm not flipping the fuck out right now." I leaned against the wood framed porch, looking out over the everglades. "I know she's alive, and Yenni said she's safe."

"But?"

"But I want her here. I want her the fuck back in Miami. I want her HERE, dammit!" I roared, throwing the glass into the murky water as the alligators started looking around. We had an electric fence surrounding the perimeter, so they didn't fuck with us like that.

"King—"

"Jaden, don't say no shit that might get you punched in the mouth, my dude."

"I'll go see if Duval need anything." He did the right thing going back inside the cabin because I had a feeling he was about to say something that might've got him accidentally killed.

"King, you can't keep going on like this," Kimbella stepped out on the porch to console me. "Cary has her own life that she wants to live. You can't get mad because that life doesn't include you."

"We were supposed to be together, Kim." I bit down on the inside of my cheek to keep calm. "She's the queen of Miami and I'm the king. Doesn't that mean we have an empire to run?"

"Not necessarily. Miami has a mayor and a city council," she joked, trying to lighten my dark mood.

I picked at a loose splinter on the porch, my mind elsewhere. "Do you know what's it's like growing up your whole life thinking it was gonna go one way and it turned out to be some other shit?"

"Actually, I do. As a creative, not only do I have a talent for etching some of the hardest designs in the world on my customers, I'm also a classically trained pianist."

"Oh yea, Ma did put you in those classes. Why you ain't do that?"

"Because when they first put me in classes, I thought that was what I wanted. Then when I started drawing those lil' fake tattoos in sixth grade, I realized I wanted to be a tattoo artist."

"And the rest is history. Why you mad?"

● ● ●

12

"You think I wanted this?" she waved a hand around in the air. "Daughter of a hood god, sister to the king of Miami? NO! I wanted to be critically acclaimed for what I did, one of the first black women to play the Palazzo Pamphili in Rome. Now I'm stuck in you and Daddy's shadow, just like Cary is."

"Cary ain't—"

"What y'all say when she got back?" Kimbella challenged. "'Oh, the queen is home.' 'Cary Muhammed' this and 'Cary Muhammed' that. Why she can't be just Cary? You don't call Duval by his first and last name! I don't see you calling up Bartholomew Hussein Palacio to go kick nobody's door in!"

"Aye, what the fuck y'all got going on out here?" Bash stormed out on the porch ready to square up.

"What's wrong with you, bro?" I couldn't help but to laugh at the look on his face from lil' sis calling him by his full name, Bash was ready to fuck some shit up.

"Y'all don't be out here telling everybody my name like that! That's only on a need-to-know basis!"

"Who she talking to, Bash?" I chuckled as he balled and un-balled his fists, trying to calm himself down. "Everybody here know your name!"

He looked around wildly for any indication that we were lying, finally satisfied Kim was being truthful. "I'm just saying, don't say that shit out loud like that."

"Don't you got a Lamaze class to go to or something?" Kim chortled. "Go back in the house!"

"Fuck you Kim. If it wasn't for your brother, you'd be one of my baby mamas too." He thumbed his nose before walking back inside as we busted out laughing.

"Like I'd really let you sniff my panties, Bartholomew! You was just eating your boogers last year, now you a hood nigga!" she called out behind him.

It was good to see them going back and forth like they always did when they were around each other, I needed that. Something to get my mind off the fact that my other half wasn't here, I needed that girl like—I ain't never felt like this about nobody. Cary needed to…nah, I needed to get my shit together.

"So this is the factory, huh." Mya's voice came from my left side. "And the only way you can get here is by boat?"

"Yea." Benny escorted her up the steps and she gave all of us a wave and a smile. "Family, this is Mya."

Tianna and Yenni glanced at her for a second with a half wave, then returned to their drinks. "Mya, do I know you?" Kimbella asked with a confused frown.

"I don't think so. Where would we know each other from though?"

"That's the thing; I don't know, but I don't forget a face," she studied her features closely. "When it come to me, I'll let you know though."

I made a mental note to keep an eye on that, because I kept telling Benny Mya was crazy, but he insisted she wasn't. Now Kimbella, my sister who was rarely in the city, knows her from somewhere. All I needed was the word and I'd pull up on her ass so quick...

"Oouu, I didn't realize it was this late!" Yenni jumped up and started walking outside. "I gotta go, see y'all later!"

"Fuck you gotta go?" Bash hopped up behind her. "All of us out here!"

"Keep telling you I ain't ya fuckin' kid, Bash!" she snatched away quick. "Ride back with one of these niggas! Better yet, get some of that pussy you out here buying bags and bundles to pull up, I'm out! Tianna, don't forget about tomorrow!"

"I won't!" Tianna snickered, waving goodbye.

"What y'all talking about?" I knew it had to do with HER, but I wanted one of them to say it. Since Yenni was gone, Tianna would talk.

"Nothing."

"Nothing, huh. This 'nothing' wouldn't have nothing to do with my girl, would it?"

"Nope." Tianna pulled a tube of lip gloss from her purse and dabbed her lips. "What, King? Go to dollfacejustbnatural.com and get you some lip stuff! They got this one scrub for smoker's lips, and if ya girl Cary is correct, you need it!" she cackled.

"So you been to Jacksonville too, huh." I couldn't believe all the women around me knew where she was and was holding out.

"Yup." She popped her lips in Duval's direction. "Got a nice house too."

"Yeen gonna give me the address though," I had to see if Tianna would give her girl up, because Yenni wasn't.

"I don't e'en know it. Anyways," she focused back on Mya. "Where you get those shoes from?"

"Oh, Benny grabbed me these from Macy's. They cute ain't they?" she modeled the sandals for everyone to see.

"Macy's huh. That's cute." Tianna stood up and pointed her manicured toes towards her fiancée, swirling her ankle back and forth. "Duval got me these from the Fendi store in Rome though. I figured I'd put 'em on for a minute before I decide I want something else though," she sighed.

"Mya ain't in to all those name brands like y'all," Benny piped up. "She can wear anything."

● ● ●
13

"Yea, I used to be like that too," Tianna popped her lips again and sat on Duval's lap. "Come over to the house, I'll give you some techniques that'll change your mind."

Cary had some techniques that changed my mind, too. Especially when she used to spread her pussy open and slide—

"King! Go home!" Kimbella snapped me out of my reverie.

"Why? What I do?"

Tianna and Mya both had their heads turned, snickering while Bash pointed at me, then dragged his finger downwards. I looked down and realized I had a hand down the front of my pants playing with my dick as thoughts of Cary weaved in and out of my mental. "Don't nobody wanna watch you beat yo' meat, nigga, this ain't PornHub!"

"Fuck y'all. Tianna wanted to see, didn't you, Tee?" I chuckled.

"No. Duval, come help me with something in the bathroom though," she snickered in his ear.

"See. You should be thanking me, not putting me out!"

"Nah, if you must know, I wanna see my man beat his while it's in me." She stood up and led him to the other side of the cabin. Watching him lick his lips as he walked behind her made me miss my lil' sexy brown thang.

"Aye, I'm out." I grabbed my keys and headed to the door as everyone else turned back to their personal conversations. These niggas didn't even tell me bye.

I didn't know about what everybody else did when they rode out to the cabin, but I took the time to think on the half mile ride from the cabin to the patch of dirt where my truck was parked. Every time I went around the fam, they always gave me those sympathy stares, as if there was anything I could have done to prevent Cary from leaving me. We could have worked it out, niggas cheat on they girl every fucking day. She wouldn't let me slide once?

She told me a little about her life in Mississippi, and the fucked up relationship she went through with that nigga Tony. I mean, this nigga had a whole ass wife, yet she was still sucking his dick faithfully. Not to mention, she used to fuck for a living. Granted, she say she did it to survive after she left her foster parents, but she had to have liked some of it, considering she did it for a year. It don't take that long to save up no money to get your own shit and do something else. Now she got morals and standards since she came back into that money. "She ain't no better than Okeema," I uttered, hitting the push button start on the whip.

I had to stop by Pop's crib to see if he had any updates on Lenore. Since she ran up on Cary that day, all of a sudden she was in the wind. It was like the bitch disappeared into thin air, ain't nobody seen or heard from her and we even had people at the airports watching. I had to make sure this time I was the one who made sure she stopped breathing, and not that nigga God.

Speaking of which, Pop never got back to me about setting up that meeting with him a few months ago. Probably because we'd gotten so busy looking for his old hoe he forgot. Only thing on his mind was getting Ma back anyway, so when I pulled up on him I made a mental note to ask him to do me that one favor. A small voice in the back of my head told me to let it go, but when I got my girl back, I didn't want to have to worry about his Creole looking, Arab ass trying to come at her.

Chapter 13

Cary

"Did he follow you out here?" I questioned Yenni as she sat at the table smashing the bowl of watermelon that I cut up for her earlier.

"Nah, Kim texted me and said he left way after I did. They had to put him out because he was sitting in that one recliner in the corner playing with his dick in front of everybody," she snickered, popping another piece of fruit in her mouth. "You should call him at least."

"Girl, fuck Leonidas." I sat down at the table across from her and stole a piece of fruit from her bowl. "I haven't thought about him in so long that I damn near forgot what he looks like."

"I know that's right," she snickered. "For real though, he walking around looking like a lost little puppy. I ain't never seen him like that, ever."

"Tell him to let Okeema come suck his dick, he'll be aight," I huffed. "That's the only reason he cheated on me in the first place."

"Because Okeema was—"

"Because I wasn't," I interrupted. "Shit, if a man love you like he say he do, you ain't gotta do shit but lay back and let him suck on yo' clit. The man is the provider, that means it's HIS job to please ME, not the other way around!"

"What?"

"He's the provider. Which means on top of him taking care of home by PROVIDING you with a roof over your head and paying all the bills, he gotta make sure you happy," I schooled. "Hell, home is where the heart is, which means if I'm his heart, I'm his home, and to make me happy, he gotta suck my pussy until I cum. Thank you for coming to today's TED talk."

"You know, I ain't never thought about it like that, but you right," Yenni sat back for a second to think, mind blown. "Atif got you over here glowing and reflecting, don't he?"

"Since I'm not under all that stress anymore, yea." I picked up her empty bowl and took it to the sink to wash it out before placing it in the dishwasher. "Leonidas and Juelz knew what Lenore was to me, yet they still allowed her to walk the streets like that shit was sweet. You know what Atif did?"

"What?"

"Dropped Lenore somewhere in the ocean about five miles from the shore."

"He…what?"

"Yup."

"When that happen?"

"Lemme tell you…"

"*You asked me a question when we first got together, and I been thinking about that answer ever since,*" Atif ran his fingertip across the tip of my nose after we got out of the shower.

"*What's that?*"

"*You asked me if I was happy, and I told you that I used to be but I'm not anymore. I wanna change my answer.*"

"*To?*"

"*I'm happy when I'm with you.*" He leaned over and planted a kiss against my cheek. "*Times like these, not when we fucking, or about to fuck, or just got done fucking. I'm happy just being with you.*"

"*Me too.*" I had to admit, I fell for him hard after that first night. We'd been inseparable since, the next day after he bought my car, he chartered a private jet for me, Yenni and Tianna to go see the orange grove my daddy bought for me outside of Jacksonville. After talking to the people that ran the property, I found out the juice from my oranges supplied half of the United States. Something told me I needed to go find out what was in that safety deposit box next.

"*Royalty told me she's not giving me a divorce,*" he sighed loudly. "*Said she was gonna fight for her marriage to the very end because she feels like we can work it out.*"

"*Can you?*"

Atif sighed before he got up and walked to look out the window of his eighty-foot yacht. "Have you even been in love with two people?"

"Yes."

His head turned sharply in my direction with an eyebrow already raised. "Who? I hope not me."

"You and Leonidas, actually."

"Well, that's to be expected, I guess." He turned back to the twinkling stars in the night sky. "I'll always have love for her for giving me my first daughter, but—"

"But what?"

"But my heart belongs to you," he spoke lowly. "Cary, you have my heart, I'll do anything for you. I haven't felt like this since—"

"Since?"

There was a long, pregnant pause between his words and I knew what he was about to say. "Since Kapri."

"We've talked about this—"

"I know, and I'm not comparing you to her. It's just that sometimes you say things, or do things that remind me of her, that's all."

"Atif, it's been five years. You married somebody else—"

"I married the rebound chick," he admitted. "You know what they say about the rebound; eventually those feelings of love wear off and you stuck with somebody you shouldn't have been with in the first place, but only stayed because they made you feel good."

"Is that what I am to you?"

"No. You mean so, so much more to me than just a fuck. With Royalty, that's all I wanted to do. I mean yea, I looked out for her family and whatnot, but shit, she worked for me first. With you though…"

"You sure this isn't a part of that hero complex of yours?" I scoffed. He told me his first wife was an arranged marriage and his second wife was in a position where she needed to be saved. With his current wife, he saved her grandmother from her grandfather, then her from her ex. And he saved me from my crazy stepmother. "Maybe you have a need to be needed."

Frozen in that moment, we both stared at each other for the longest time as he pondered my words. "So you don't think a man who needs to be needed can fall in love then, huh."

"Honestly, I don't know. I'm just a girl from Miami missing her daddy and trying to find myself," I admitted. "Trying to see who I am without everyone around me telling me who I should be."

"I don't know your full background, Cary." Atif took a seat at the foot of the bed and reached around for my feet, kneading my toes *one by one. "I don't know why your stepmother has so much animosity towards you, I don't know the history you have with Leonidas and his family...I don't know anything more than what you tell me. So if you tell me you can't do this with me anymore, all I can do is respect your word and back down. But I will tell you this, love." He scooted closer and pressed his lips against my forehead with the utmost of care. "Everybody needs somebody to protect them from something, even if it's from themselves."*

In that very moment, his words shook me to my foundation. Nobody ever told me I needed to be protected from myself. I laid in that bed and thought about my actions towards others and how I allowed myself to be treated since my daddy died. A part of me still blamed myself for Myron raping me, I could have done something to stop it. After the first time he got me pregnant, I could've said something to the woman at the abortion clinic when she asked if someone touched me, I could have ran away. Working the truck stops, I didn't have to sell myself for a whole year with nothing to show for it but a couple of dollars and a sore pussy at the end of the night.

When I got to Mississippi, I should have been on my feet a lot sooner than two years, but I didn't want to. I wanted someone to take care of me like my daddy did. Even after I got my job, I didn't have to prostitute myself to keep it. I could have recorded Tony when he demanded that I suck his dick in his office and got him fired. There was so much more that I could have done with my life, considering who I was. To be someone that the city of Miami always called a queen, even in my absence, I was anything but. And why was that? I had nobody to protect me from the thoughts that ran rampant in my head.

"Atif."

"Yes, love?"

"Can you do something for me?"

"Name it."

"Lenore—"

"I'll have her at the docks waiting for you when we get back. You can decide how you wanna handle that…"

"So how did you handle it?" Yenni was enraptured by the story of how Lenore finally met her demise.

"Dang, can I finish?" I chuckled…

We got back from out late night cruise and instead of going to his truck, we detoured to an area where the freighters picked up the containers to be carried out to sea. Atif took me three rows back to a container that had a guard at the entrance and two on the roof. "What do you need?"

"Let me have a conversation with her first," I peeked around the back of the container to ensure we were alone. "Maybe we can be two rational adults about this whole thing."

● ● ●

Atif nodded to the man in front of the door and after he opened the iron entrance, I stepped aside. Unable to see anything until my eyes adjusted to the darkness, the stench hit me before I saw her crouched in the middle of the container shivering. "Lenore."

"Cary, please tell them this was all a mistake! PLEASE!"

"I'm not understanding which one of us made the mistake though," I took a deep breath in before I covered my nose and walked inside. "You told me my father was senile when he put my name on everything he owned..."

"Cary, I swear...I PROMISE! I'll go away...far, far away and you'll never see me again! Please just let me go!"

Now see, she wasn't talking none of that when Benny snatched her up. I wonder what changed. "I can't do that, Lenore. See, it was bad enough you conspired against my daddy, but to find out you killed my mother too...ain't no coming back from that."

"Cary, from the bottom of my heart to the depths of my soul, I AM SORRY!" she cried. "There's nothing...NOTHING I can say or do to bring your parents back, but I promise if you let me go, I'll..."

"Atif, I'm ready!"

My baby came to stand by my side with a machete in hand and a Kool-Aid smile on his face. "You need this?"

Lenore let out a scream that would've shook the average person down to their very soul, but that shit didn't faze me. My mind went

• • •
14

back to a day when I was about eight years old and we were arguing. I told her my real mother wouldn't do the things she did and I guess she got in her feelings. She snatched the one picture I had of my mother, the only picture of her Daddy still had, off of the fireplace and tossed it in the flames because of her hatred for me. "Yea."

"God, God, God…" Lenore mumbled over and over again with her eyes closed as if she was praying. "Why are you not showing me mercy? I said three hail Gods…"

"Ha, you funny." Atif snickered, watching me twirl the machete like a drum major. "I ain't got no control over what you got going on with her."

"You won't let me repent? PLEASE GOD, LET ME REPENT!" she pleaded.

"Yea, though I walk through the valley of the shadow of death, I will fear no evil for thou art with me. Thy rod and thy staff, they comfort me," I began, twirling faster.

"GOD PLEASE!"

"Blame this one on the son of the morning," I gritted. Swiping the machete across her neck, I severed her head from the rest of her body. Lenore's blood splashed against both of us as her body sat for a few seconds more, then pitched forward to rest on the wooden floor. "Bitch."

"Felt good, didn't it?" Atif whispered in my ear.

"I'm ready to fuck now. Get the men to clean this shit up."

"Mmhmm..." he growled, grabbing my ass as we walked out the container together.

"DIZZAM, CARY!" Yenni jumped up for the table with a hand over her mouth. "So she dead-dead, huh!"

"Yup." My phone started buzzing across the table, so I grabbed it before it hit the floor. "Hey Atif."

"What you doing?"

"Trying to go out on the boat tonight. What you doing?"

"Making sure the staff got the boat cleaned to your standards," he chuckled with that mischievous twinkle in his eye. I loved the fact that he would Face Time me so I could watch his lips move when he spoke. "What time am I picking you up?"

"Same time. Or I can meet you—"

"Don't insult me like that. I'll be there at 8:45. Tell Yenni I got a friend for her, he'll be here tomorrow."

"K. Love you."

"Love you too, sexy," he smiled one more time before he hung up.

"Is he still married?"

"They're battling it out in court. She said he can have everything, but she wants to keep custody of their daughter."

"No shared custody?"

"She wants full custody. No visitation, no nothing. Oh, but she does want spousal and child support though."

"Lemme get this straight: the man can't see his child, but he better take care of her? What type of Divorce Court bullshit is that?" Yenni griped.

"Exactly. Sometimes he just looks so sad when I see him, like he has the weight of the world on his shoulders." Today was the first time I saw him smile since they started their divorce proceedings. I wanted to tell him to call it off, but he was determined to see it through. A part of me felt bad because I was breaking up a happy home, but according to him it hadn't been happy in a while.

"Be careful, Cary. I know he said you wasn't the rebound, but is he yours? Don't have that man divorce his wife because you said so then you turn around and leave him because you decided you still love King."

"That's the thing though, Yenni."

"What's the thing?"

"I don't. I don't love Leonidas."

"Well maybe you should tell him that before you bump into him somewhere, considering you haven't left Miami."

"Yea, well, I don't owe him any more than he owes me. We're even. And for the first time since my daddy died, I'm happy." I went to straighten the small pile of mail on the end table next to the front door.

"Are you?"

"Why wouldn't I be?"

"So you mean to tell me you're happy being the side chick to a married man," Yenni frowned.

"I told you in the beginning, I wanted Atif. I would've been fine as long as he was in my life some kind of way and he is. He's done way more for me than Leonidas, who knew what hotel I was at and didn't pull up not once. Didn't even call the hotel to make sure I made it, nor did he call up to the room to make sure I was good, knowing I didn't have a phone. I could've been over there starving to death and he didn't care. Atif, on the other hand, took care of me when he didn't have to. Still is, he went half on this house. So if that's what I get for being a side chick, sign me the fuck up!" I spat.

"Don't shoot the messenger, love," Yenni held her hands up defensively in front of her baby bump. "I'm just looking out for your well-being. But know too, if I gotta go up against your lil' boyfriend for you, one of us is gonna die. You make the call on which one of us that is."

"Yenni, don't talk like that—"

"If he breaks your heart, Cary…" she paused for a second so she didn't bust out crying with her emotional ass, "I'm not gonna be responsible for what I do to him or Pauper."

"Pauper?"

"Yea. Ain't that his wife's name?"

"Girl, shut up!" I cackled.

"What's so funny? That ain't her—"

"Yenni, who the fuck gonna name they daughter Pauper?" I fell out laughing at her goofy ass. "Her name is Royalty."

"What-the-fuck-ever," she waved, rolling her eyes in the process. "Anyway, you know Mya, right?"

"Mmhmm."

"Benny brought her to the factory."

"For what." We both walked through my bedroom to the walk in closet so I could find something to wear. I ran my hand across the cherry wood dresser in the middle of the closet as Yenni checked out my shoe wall.

"I don't know. Kimbella said she knows her from somewhere though."

"Hmpf." I went back and forth between some booty shorts and a tank top to a dress that barely covered my ass. When we went out on the boat, Atif and I watched the sun set behind the ocean, got drunk and fucked. It had been a while since we did all that, especially since he had so much going on, but tonight I had plans to remind him of how overdue I was for real. I was about to get cute to go get ate out...I meant go out to eat on Atif's yacht.

"Cary."

"Huh."

"I said what has your girl been up to since y'all used to work together?"

"Oh. Uhmm...I don't know."

"How is she your friend and you don't know?" Yenni snapped.

"Just like Leonidas was still fucking his ex when he was telling me he was going to find Lenore. Just like his father lied to me about not knowing where I was. Just like how fucked up my whole life has been up to this point because nobody thought I should know the truth about my legacy. That's how I didn't know." I spoke calmly, not allowing the shit to affect me. Wasn't nothing I could do about it, why be mad?

"Cary, I need you to get it together." She shook her head and walked out of my expansive closet that Atif already filled up with clothes, shoes, and lingerie. "You can't be THIS happy with a married man you just met—"

"Why can't I? Because I'm supposed to be miserable with Leonidas? Knowing he strayed, yet forgiving him so he can do it again? At least I know what I'm getting into with Atif, he's always been honest with me from the beginning. I made the choice to see where this goes, not having someone make it for me then get mad because I don't wanna play no more. Why do I have to be the bigger person? I got feelings too! FUCK LEONIDAS!" I roared.

"This ain't about Leonidas! It's about you! Cary, you losing yourself in this man and—"

"I'll see you tomorrow, Yenni."

"Oh, now I gotta go?"

"Yenni please. I love you, but I don't wanna say nothing to you that I can't take back because I'm mad."

"Naw, gon' say what you gotta say, Cary! Say what you gotta say!" she taunted, her little belly bouncing up and down every time she jumped in my face.

"Bye Yenni."

"Say it, Cary! SAY IT!"

"I'll have you escorted outta here if you don't leave!"

"Fuck you, Cary! Fuck you and this house! Now I see why King was still fucking Okeema, that bitch know her place! Obviously yo' bougie ass don't!"

"Leonidas still fucking Pickmesha because she don't give a fuck about herself! At least I have some fucking standards!"

"Standards?" she chuckled bitterly as she snatched her keys off the table near the door, knocking over my mail. "You fucking a married man, fuck you know about standards!"

"And you pregnant by the community hoe!" I snapped. "Bash got twenty fucking kids, no cap! Got you out here thinking he bout to marry you, he just don't wanna let the pussy go! Congratulations baby mama number twenty fucking one!"

"FUCK YOU CARY! I HOPE THAT MAN LEAVE YO' ASS JUST LIKE YO' MAMA AND YO' DADDY DID!" Yenni screamed as she walked through the front door. "DON'T NOBODY WANT YOU, YOU COULDN'T EVEN HOLD ON TO THE ONE NIGGA YOU HAD! GO BACK TO MISSISSIPPI AND GOBBLE UP A DICK, YOU NASTY HOE!" she roared before slamming the door shut.

Her words still hurt long after she was gone. I told her...I told her to leave. I told her to just leave...why didn't she? Why didn't she leave like I told her to? Why…why would she say that to me? I told her to leave…I told her to leave…I told her to leave…

Atif found me in the closet sitting on the floor crying while rocking back and forth hugging my knees. "Cary?"

"Why didn't she leave when I told her to, Atif? Why didn't she leave?" I sobbed with fresh tears.

"Who, Yenni?"

"She…" I sniffed, "She said…"

"Shhh, I got you. I got you, Cary," he sat on the floor with me, rocking back and forth with his arms around my body. "Shhh…don't worry about what she said…it's ok…it's ok…"

We stayed like that for the longest time, long enough for me to fall asleep cradled in his arms. At some point he picked me up and carried me to bed, wiping my face with a cool towel before he tucked me in. I couldn't believe Yenni would say those things, even after I practically begged her to leave. Funny, because this whole thing started over her not liking the fact that I was dating Atif, yet he was the one here to wipe my tears away. It seemed like everyone wanted me to stay away from him, yet he was here for me when they abandoned me. Atif was all I had.

Chapter 14

Leonidas

"Yenni, slow down! I can't hear you! What did you say?"

"Cary ain't in no fucking Jacksonville! She right here in Miami!" Yenni yelled over the wind blowing in the background. "I just left that bitch house and I'm on the causeway right now!"

"You the one who said she was in Jacksonville though, Yenni—"

"I LIED! That bitch...out here...on..." Yenni's voice went in and out before the phone suddenly went dead. I tried calling her back and the call went straight to voicemail, so I called Jaden to see if he could use her phone number to pull her last known GPS location and waited for him to call me back.

"This bitch," Okeema groaned instead of sucking my dick. "We back to this again?"

"Fuck is you talmbout? You know that's the queen!"

"I know you been here for the past two months too!" she spat. "Lying, telling me everything I wanna hear! 'Oh, fuck Cary!' 'I was sicka her anyway!' Oh, and my personal favorite? 'Now that she gone, let's raise our baby together!' Yenni call and soon as you hear her name, it's fuck Okeema though, right? I'm not gonna keep doing this with you!"

"Then don't!" I snapped back. "You knew what it was! You knew what was up!"

Okeema got off her knees and started looking around for her clothes. "Sicka this shit with you and this bitch," she grumbled. "By the way, where's my auntie, King?"

"Your who?"

"My auntie, dammit! I haven't seen or heard from her in over a month!"

"So? That's a grown woman, maybe she went and found her own dick for a change," I snickered to myself. "Got tired of fucking with everybody else's."

"I swear to God, if I find out you did something to her because of that bitch…"

I pulled out an eighth of premium gas and rolled up, this girl wasn't about to start stressing me out. *Here go this nigga name on the lips of yet another bitch I'm fucking. This clown wanna be me so bad…* "Thought you was leaving."

"Stop calling me! I don't wanna see you, hear from you…nothing until after I have this baby!" she snapped, storming towards the door.

"I'll see you tomorrow. Have that pussy fresh next time, don't come over here smelling like a lobster lover's dream!"

• • •
15

"Bitch, I know somebody that like it…ooop, your father!" she yelled out before slamming the door.

I thought she was lying about being pregnant, but Okeema definitely had a pudge. Baby even moved sometimes when we was fucking, I got kicked a couple of times by its lil' ass. Whether it was my seed or my sibling didn't matter, I still didn't want it's mother. She served her purpose every time we met up.

Jaden hit my line as soon as I heard Okeema's truck pull out of the parking lot. "King."

"Yea."

"I haven't been able to pick up the signal to exactly where she was, but I can tell you the GPS had her somewhere off of Venetian Way. Want me to ride out there?"

Cary ain't in no fucking Jacksonville! She right here in Miami… Yenni sounded like she was pissed for some reason, but at the moment I didn't care. "Nah. Aye, see if you can pull up any cameras in the area. Hack into somebody's security system if you have to."

"What am I looking for?"

"Cary Muhammed." I had something for her muthafuckin' ass. Got me out here worried to death on whether or not she was ok up in Jacksonville and she hadn't left the city? Fuck she on.

"I'm on it."

I waited for him to hang up and scrolled through my contacts looking for another number. "Aye."

"King."

"You miss me?"

"A little. Why?" LaLa, the bottle girl who worked at the strip club, popped her lips in my ear.

"My dick said he miss you. Won't you come over here and talk to him for a lil' bit so he can feel better."

"You be actin' too shady for me," she sighed. "One minute you taking me shopping, next minute you in your feelings about your ex and I don't wanna hear that shit."

"I ain't in my feelings about her now." *Especially since I'm 'bout to get her back.* "You don't miss me?"

"You coming to pick me up?"

"Didn't I just get your car fixed the other day?"

"Damn, King! You can't come out here and get me?"

"I'll send you an Uber, but naw. I'm comfortable." I grunted.

"Pussy ass niggas! Always wanna fuck but can't—"

LaLa had to get hung up on after that one, if I wanted to hear a bitch nagging in my ear I'd call Okeema back. Jaden needed to give me some kinda update and soon.

My text ringer dinged and I ignored it, this lil' bitch ain't have the pussy like that for me to be going back and forth with her if she wasn't fucking. She said it herself: I was always talking about my ex who wasn't really my ex. Me and Cary was on a break, like them bitches be saying about they nigga when he go off to fuck his new bitch on an island somewhere. *This lil' hoe bout to get on my muthafuckin' nerves,* I thought, snatching the phone from off the bed.

Opening my text messages, I saw it wasn't her, Jalen was sending me pics he pulled off of Cary's neighbor's security cameras who I guess lived across the street. First pic was of Cary smiling as she stepped out of a car I know I didn't buy. The more I scrolled through the pics of the jet black metallic 2021 Panamera 4 with tinted windows with that gunmetal gray Range Rover parked behind it in the driveway, the more incentive I had to get my ass up and drive down to Venetian Way to ride up and down the street until I found that house. Cary left ME for HIM? I knew she didn't up and leave me on her own. And with HIM of all people? Nah. We was about to get this shit squared away TONIGHT.

Cary

"What was that?"

"Hmm?"

BAM! BAM! BAM! Somebody was beating on my front door like they were the police. That didn't happen in this neighborhood. "Atif—"

He jumped out of bed before I could finish my sentence, grabbing his pistol from the end table. "I'm on it, baby."

I grabbed my black silk robe from the foot of the bed and wrapped it around my body. Running a hand through my hair, I looked around the room to see what time it was. *Who the hell is that beating on my door at 3 a.m.?*

"Let me in this muthafuckin' house! My bitch in here, so technically this my shit anyway!" Leonidas? How did he find— woooow, Yenni really broke girl code like that?

"First and foremost, don't no bitches live here! Second, ain't shit over here 'technically' yours when half of it belongs to me! Just like everything and everybody in this muthafucka!" Atif yelled back. I should've been mad…for real…but for some reason the way he said that shit was sexy as hell.

"Oh, so that's how you took my bitch from me? Buying her shit?" Leonidas retorted. "You ain't doin' shit I ain't already did!"

I couldn't help but to crack a smile when Atif started laughing at my ex; Leonidas was so serious and Atif was so laid back. "Yea, that condo down the street from you was cute, in an insecure nigga kind of way," he snickered. "You got a woman you call your 'queen' waiting on you to pull up like she ain't allowed to go nowhere without you. And to top it all off, you left her vulnerable—"

"Who you talkin' to? How the fuck you gonna tell me—"

"Because Juelz called ME," Atif's voice was commanding on its own, baby didn't even have to raise it for somebody to understand what he meant. "Obviously, he didn't trust YOU to do a man's job. Not to mention, how was this woman still breathing when both of y'all knew she had beef with Cary?"

"Aye, you ain't bout to—"

"Nah, YOU ain't bout to call yourself chastising me," Atif continued. "I ain't one of the niggas that work for you, just because we standing here talking don't think yo' ass can't get killed. We having this conversation out of respect for the queen of the castle."

"I ain't bout to be having this conversation with you! CARY! Tell my bitch to come outside!" Leonidas roared.

"You should call her tomorrow. Oh wait, she didn't give you the new number after I bought the phone, huh. Well, stop by early, we usually have a sunrise breakfast on the yacht, but since we didn't spend the night on the water we might be leaving here at about 7 a.m. Think you can make it?"

"I'm killing you, my nigga. And it ain't cause of that bitch either," Leonidas growled from outside on the porch.

"I'll be looking forward to it. In the meantime," Atif slammed the door in King's face before he turned back to me. "This who you wanted to spend your life with? I mean damn, I know I'm married, but you can do so much better."

BOOM! The alarm on my car started screaming through the neighborhood when a second BOOM! sounded off right after it. I peeked out the window to see Leonidas's car speeding off down the street and both of our vehicles had the decorative pavers from my front lawn tossed through our windshields. "What the fu—"

"See how bitches act?" Atif's breath was cool on the back of my neck with his man pole smashed up against my booty cheeks. "A man would've cut his losses. Now I gotta show him how a bully from the Chi gets down."

"Atif—"

"I'm not gonna do nothing to him…yet. But he is gonna pay for that windshield one way or the other," he murmured on his way back to bed. "Come rub my back."

Taking one last glance out the front window, I ran to catch up with my man. Leonidas better come with a whole army if he was gonna go up against Atif. After all, the streets did call him God.

Chapter 15

Leonidas

"You need an army of niggas? For what?" Pop demanded to know.

"Does it matter? Call Estevan—"

"Nah, if I make that call, it better be a life or death situation," Pop went back to smoking his after breakfast cigar. "And if it's a life or death situation, you need to tell me why and you need to tell me now."

"Fuck it. Maggie gave me her number, so I'll call him myself, I grunted, walking out of his study. I threw a few bricks through a few windows a few nights ago because I was pissed, and now every time I turn around, something else going on.

First my Benz wouldn't start. Got it towed to the dealer, only for them to tell me somebody emptied ten pounds of sugar in my gas tank and fucked up my engine. I went to get the rental, later on that day somebody flattened all four tires. Call the insurance company to make a claim, all of a sudden my policy was cancelled. They said they could reinstate it, but it wouldn't cover the flat tires. This shit had the God written all over it.

Even still, she wasn't back. I tried to call Yenni to see what happened between her and Cary, and she wasn't talking. Tianna rolled her eyes at me every time I pulled up at Duval's, so I knew she still wasn't saying shit. Whatever they had going on between them was between them, I just wanted a few minutes alone with Cary to talk.

"Aye King," Mya walked up on me at Auto Zone when I was looking for a locking fuel cap. Mercedes was trying to charge me out the ass for one and somebody told me I could find them cheaper up here. "I been meaning to ask you: you seen Cary?"

I wish muthafuckas would stop asking me about that damn girl. "Nah, I ain't seen her in a minute. Why, what's good?"

"Nothing, Last time we met up she was saying we needed to get caught up and I haven't seen her since. Thought I would be able to catch her out there at the factory, but she wasn't there either," she replied, looking lost.

"Wish I could help you, but I can't." I found what I was looking for and headed to the registers.

"Did y'all ever find Lenore?" she wanted to know.

"Actually, nah. I think she probably went back to—shit!"

"What? What did I say?"

I paid for the gas cap with one hand and texted Pop with the other as I walked out the store and to my whip:

King: *Where did you say God was from?*

Pop: *Chicago. Why?*

● ● ●
16

King: *And Lenore had people out there too, right?*

Pop: *You think they some kin?*

King: *I don't know, but check on that for me, aight?*

Pop*: On it*

God made it a point to bring up Okeema when I first met him, how he know anything about her unless he knew Lenore? Pop ain't out here telling my business like that. *Wouldn't it be some shit if he already knew who Cary was when he pulled up on her?* I wondered aloud, tossing the gas cap in the passenger seat. What do this dude want for real?

‡

"I'm surprised to be hearing from you so soon," Maggie seemed calm considering it was me calling and not Pop. "How's my favorite niece?"

"That's what I was calling about, Auntie." I took a deep breath in and blew it out, only because I promised her I would be careful with Cary's heart and I wasn't. "She left."

"Oh, is she on her way back down here?"

"No, she left me."

"Oh."

Oh? "Auntie am I missing something?"

"No, no Leonidas." Maggie's voice didn't match her words, almost as if she was covering something up. "Tell me what happened."

I told her everything, from the time Cary got snatched up until now. I even told her about me and Okeema and the God going to rescue her, in case she went back to tell her husband what we talked about. "King, what did we discuss before you left? What did we talk about?"

"Auntie, I know I fucked up—"

"You did more than fuck up. You gave her the opportunity to confide in another man."

"No I didn't. If she had a problem with me, she could've called Yenni. Ain't that what women do?"

"That's where you're wrong, Leonidas. You can't treat Cary like she's the same as other women when that's not how she was raised, that's not how she was built. She spent a lot of time in survivor mode, so now she's coming into the woman we taught her to be. What she does is go to a man to get their opinion on why her man is acting the way he does. If that man's explanation makes sense, she'll either come back or leave. In your case, it really didn't take too much."

I listened to her words with my head down in my chest, all this time I been blaming the God when this was all me. "Auntie what am I supposed to do?"

"You say she's seeing someone else?"

"Yea. Some dude that calls himself—"

"God." She finished. "Estevan and I know Atif's father."

"Who is Atif?"

"You know him as God. We know him as Atif."

"He ain't from here, is he?"

"No, Atif's family is from Armenia. Well, his father is. Aram is also a wanted man on four continents."

"What, the United States, Canada, Mexico—"

"No, Leonidas," Maggie snickered. "Four CONTINENTS. Europe, Africa, North and South America."

"Ahhh, ok—"

"Leonidas, I'm warning you. Do NOT mess with this man. Aram Hermes is dangerous and so is his son. WE don't have the firepower to go up against him and his family. If you lost Cary to Atif, cut your losses and move forward. You know how the old saying goes."

"Nah, I don't."

"If you love someone, set them free. If they come back, you'll be together forever. If they don't they were never yours to begin with."

"Auntie, she is mine. She gonna ALWAYS be mine—"

"Yet look how you handled her," Maggie interrupted viciously. "Like she's one of your little Miami hoochies. You don't treat a queen like a peasant then get mad because she knows her worth."

I should've called Unc because Maggie was digging in my shit with no Vaseline. "You right, Auntie."

"I know I'm right, dammit. Now, if she does talk to you, let her speak first so you can get a feel for where her head is. If she's with Atif though…" Maggie let out a deep sigh and I imagined her shaking her head.

"If she's with Atif then what?"

"She's gone already. Atif has a penchant for dark skinned women, and one with Cary's beauty…you never should've let that happen, Leonidas."

"I didn't! That was Pop's bright idea!" I snapped.

"Juelz?"

"Yea! We was at the cabin when he found out Lenore kidnapped her from the house—"

"From YOUR house?"

"Nah, we was at Cary's spot."

"Then what did Juelz do?" she questioned curiously.

"Said he had to call in a hitta, and that's who he called."

Maggie held the phone for a long time, I had to check and make sure she hadn't hung up. "Yea, so make sure you take my advice Leonidas. I gotta go, call me and let me know how it went," she rushed off the phone.

The fuck was that all about?

Chapter 16

Juelz

"Hello?"

"Really, Juelz? You sent Atif to rescue Cary from Lenore? REALLY JUELZ?"

"Maggie, what was I supposed to do? It was either send Atif out there so he would leave us alone or pay interest on that money from back in the day! I don't know about you and Estevan, but I ain't got it like that no more!" I snapped.

"You could have talked to Aram—"

"Yea?" I chuckled bitterly. "How you think that was gonna go, negotiating with a man who basically said have his money or he killing your entire family? Burning down everything you own! All over a deal you knew nothing about that he had with a dead man! Ahseir put us in this bind, he ain't here to get us out! Hell yea I sent his son to rescue Cary! It was either her or me!"

"What happened to honor and loyalty, Juelz? What ever happened to family?" Maggie gritted in my ear.

I pushed the cigar butts around in the ashtray until I found one that looked like I could still get a few puffs off of it. "Ahseir knew what he did."

"That was over twenty-five years ago, Juelz! He didn't even know the truth when he died!"

"I don't give a fuck, Maggie! Just because he didn't know the truth don't mean he ain't pull no dirty shit! I'm glad that nigga dead!"

"Juelz, you need to grow up. And if you don't soon, I pray God has mercy on your soul," Maggie's words were ominous coming through the phone, as if she knew something I didn't.

"Don't preach that bullshit to me. Matter of fact, get the fuck off my phone." I hung up in her face so I could finish making some arrangements. I hadn't heard from my bottom bitch in a minute, and my wife was still in Cali. Bottom bitch number two was gonna have to do, I needed my dick sucked too.

As soon as I picked up the phone to call her, she rang my phone. "Juelz."

"What you doing?"

"Nothing right now, why?"

"Come suck my dick."

"On my way. By the way, your son didn't give me any money—"

• • •
16

Whatever Okeema had going on with King was between her and King, I ain't have nothing for her but some hard dick. "Hurry the fuck up, he waiting."

"Ok."

I knew she was still fucking my son, but I didn't give a fuck. A hoe gonna do whatever she need to do to survive, and I was gonna nut all over her tonsils so she could keep living. That baby could've been mine, King's, or the next nigga's kid and I was still skeeting on his forehead since she couldn't get pregnant twice. Sometimes I closed my eyes and pictured she was my wife when I was in them guts, but lately Cary's face been popping up when I fucked Okeema. I knew the God was gonna take her from my son and hoped he'd let me get some appreciation pussy too.

Wrong or right, Cary wasn't my biological daughter. I watched her in the shower when she came over here that first time, which was why I stayed in my study while my wife was around. I hadn't seen her in a few years, and Lenore hadn't either since she was tricking off with that producer. Cary was a new and improved version of her mother and I wanted her. First time when Lenore popped up at her spot I didn't know nothing about, but this last time she got kidnapped I paid her to do so. I figured I'd get a two for one special: fuck her like her father fucked my wife and popped her off with my twins.

Kimbella and Kourtne'a were not my daughters, biologically they were Cary's sisters. Ahseir didn't know, and had Kourtne'a not needed a blood transfusion when she wrapped her first car around a light pole in Miami Beach, Judy would've never told me about the drunken night when my so-called 'best friend' raped her. Of course I forgave her, it wasn't her fault my right hand was slimy like that, but he knew full well what he did.

My wife told me she was at his house with Christina listening to the new Jodeci CD and drinking. By the time Ahseir came in, they were drunk and reminiscing. Christina passed out first, and when Ahseir came back from taking a piss, he saw his lady laid out on the floor snoring. He grabbed Judy's hand, pulled her up off the floor, took her to the kitchen and made his move. When she told him no, he took advantage. Afterwards, he went in the bathroom, washed up, and went to bed, leaving her on the kitchen floor confused and alone. She cleaned herself up and put it in the back of her mind, next thing we knew she was pregnant. It never dawned on her that Ahseir might be the twins father, but when the hospital ran the tests on my blood and told me I wasn't a match to the girls who I raised all of their lives as my own, she finally broke down and admitted her dark secret.

I go to that man's grave and piss on it once a month. Leonidas is my son, but the two girls who call me daddy aren't. I could never tell them the truth about their father, so I let it ride. According to the Good Book, sins of the father are passed down to the child upon his death, and Cary got to atone for her father's sins. Truthfully, I expected the God to have her strung out by now, but I forgot he like 'em dark skinned. I bet the pussy good too, hate that I didn't get to taste that when she used to work at the truck stops. Lenore got top dollar for it when she sold her to Myron and Kimoyrah, wish it was me. That caseworker owed her some money for them pills, so she set it up for them to legally adopt her stepdaughter. Since Lenore was her guardian on record, she signed the paperwork for them to do so.

I couldn't get at Cary, but I did get to sample something: Mya Denise. Every time she used to come to my house when they were younger, I would touch her little bud when nobody was looking. I would catch her eyeballing my son and knew she was ready, so I made my move. The day I overheard her ask Leonidas if she could suck his dick was after I introduced her mouth to mine. I taught her everything she knew, then she ran away when her mother started suspecting her of fucking somebody. Which we hadn't, but in order for her to do what I want, I had to lie a little. I told her I was getting her an apartment and then we could fuck. In the meantime, she let me suck on that lil' teenage pussy of hers and it was so sweet. She was ready.

From the moment I slid my dick inside Mya's tight walls, I knew she would be in love. And every time I did, I wished she was Cary. Ahseir had people watching his daughter like a hawk up until he died, and she went into foster care right after that. Lenore wouldn't give me Myron's address, and even if she had, he wasn't giving her up either. That one night when they shut down the truck stop because that girl died, I went up there drunk looking for Cary:

"I said where the fuck is Cary!" The girl in front of me looked like her from the back, but when she turned around I saw she wasn't. "Bitch you betta tell me which one of these niggas fucking my pussy right now!" I growled in her ear.

"I swear I don't know!" lil' hoe screamed. "She was out here a few minutes ago and now she gone! Please don't kill me!"

With my hand wrapped around her neck, I thought about all those times when Cary was younger and I had the perfect opportunity to make my move but didn't. When Ahseir would drop her off at the house for sleepovers with the twins. When Judy would go pick her up because she was pissed off at Lenore. That one year I dressed up as Santa Claus and she sat on my lap for over an hour telling me what she wanted for Christmas as her father argued back and forth with his wife. I could have made my move and didn't.

"I...I can't...I can't breathe..." I heard as fingernails clawed at my fist. Realizing where I was, I dropped the lil' hoe on the ground and went to look for who I really wanted to fuck.

"Juelz," Lenore's voice came from behind me. "What you doing down here slumming? Much money as you got, go buy you some top shelf pussy."

"Nah, there's some top shelf down here that I want—"

● ● ●

"Oh, we can go to your car," she began, rubbing a hand across my chest.

"Not you, bitch. Some tight pussy down here—"

"You ain't gonna find too much tight pussy out here," she giggled hoeishly. "Unless you want one of these lil' runaways."

"Where they—" We both turned towards the high pitched scream coming from the eighteen-wheeler where I dropped the lil' hoe to the ground a few minutes earlier. "SHIT! Aye, I gotta go, call me tomorrow, aight?"

"The hell is going on over here now?" Lenore grumbled. "Yea, I'll call you tomorrow, lemme go see what these damn—"

"Lenore! LENORE!" someone screamed as I walked briskly to my trap car and got the fuck outta dodge.

Don't get me wrong, I'm not like that, I guess you could say I got a screw loose somewhere. Never would I have done something like that to Kimbella or Kourtne'a, but it was something about Mya and Cary that I had to have. At this point in my life I knew I couldn't, but damn if a nigga dick didn't get hard thinking about them.

I heard somebody tapping on my front door and checked the outside cameras from the monitor in my office. Okeema stood in front of the door adjusting her lip gloss, like that shit wasn't gonna be wrapped around the base of my dick in five minutes. As I made

● ● ●
17

my way downstairs, I thought about that night when it was Cary and Benny on the monitor. Yea, I sent Judy to break that shit up, he was looking too comfortable. I knew that look in his eyes because I used to have it myself when I looked at her. Nah, we was gonna keep that one in the family too.

"Took you long enough," Okeema slouched in the house pouting and rubbing her baby bump. "I'm hungry."

King would've never found out I hit his old work off had she not left that pregnancy test in the drawer of his nightstand. She did that shit on purpose too, knowing he'd find it. See, King thought she got pregnant that night he brought her over, but nah. Sis got pregnant two weeks before that when Judy went back to Belize to visit her family and I turned the cameras off in the house.

"Shoulda' got you something to eat before you got here, fuck I look like going grocery shopping for you?" I spat back. "It's some oranges in the refrigerator, grab one and bring yo' ass on. Told you I'm ready to get my dick sucked, coming over here talmbout you hungry. Fuck I look like."

"Gee, lemme see…you look like the nigga that got me pregnant!" she snapped off. "I ain't do this by myself!"

"And I told you to take care of that shit!" I clapped back. "I know my son gave you some abortion money! Hell, it still ain't too late!"

"I ain't aborting a muthafuckin' thing! You gonna take care of my baby, dammit!"

"Bitch I should—" I raised a hand to slap some sense into her and stopped. If I did that, I wouldn't get no head. "Damn. I'm sorry, Keema. I shouldn't be raising a hand to you, but you just be pissing me the fuck off sometimes."

"I know, Juelz." She fell for that same ass line every time. "And I know it's just too much going on right now, I should be your peace, not your problem."

I sat down on the couch and unbuttoned my pants in the process. "Mmhmm."

"Juelz, I'm hungry for real though," she spoke softly as she got down on her knees and unzipped my pants. "Can you get me something to eat before we do this?"

"I'll get you something from Uber Eats, I promise." I ran my fingers through her hair as she pulled out my meat and leaned forward with her mouth open.

"Can I get some—"

I grabbed the back of her head and shoved her lips around the tip, adjusting myself so she could show him the attention he deserved. "Make me cum and get anything you want," I wheezed. Soon as my eyes closed, Cary's face popped up on the back of my eyelids. "Yea baby…just like that…take care of…SHIT!"

Chapter 17

Cary

Atif and I had just got back from a vineyard in Vero Beach when he said he needed to stop off somewhere in Coral Gables. I'd never been wine tasting before, and I loved everything he did to make me more well-rounded and cultured. It wasn't always about hitting the blocks and shooting at people, nor was it all about killing my enemies off one by one. I was a queen, and a rich one at that. It was time for me to start doing something different than laying in bed fucking and getting fucked back. I had to work on me if I was ever going to be something to someone else.

We were walking down the street when I saw signage for the bank where my father supposedly had something tucked away in a safe deposit box with my name on it. I stopped short when Atif gently pulled me towards him, nervous as hell. "Is this the bank?"

"This is it. Apollo Bank, right?"

"What you think is in the safe deposit box though?" I whispered as he held the door open for me.

"I don't know. Like I said, I never met your father, he dealt with Pop."

"Hi, and welcome to Apollo Bank," the drab lady standing at the front door eased over to help us with her nose turned up. I guess it was an anomaly to see wealthy Black people in Coral Gables that weren't drug dealers or celebrities. "How may I assist?"

"Yes, I—"

"Are you a personal banker?" Atif took control, like he usually did.

"No, but if you can tell me why you would require a personal— "

"We don't deal with the hired help." Atif led me to a chair in the waiting area and waited until I sat before he did.

"Sir, banking requirements are—"

"Get your manager over here if you have a problem with a customer who has assets IN THIS BANK taking a seat while she waits to be serviced." Atif casually picked up a banking magazine from the table and leisurely thumbed through the pages. "You still standing here?"

"I…I uhmm…" she stuttered, flustered.

"NOW, Matilda F.!" he snapped as she scurried away.

"You wrong for scaring that woman like that," I giggled. "She just doing her job."

"Fuck her. She took too damn long," he grumbled. "I wanted her to jump like she do when Yaacob come in here, ain't nobody got time for her bullshit."

See, that's what I loved about Atif, even when he was serious he kept a smile on my face. He looked up from the magazine when he heard me giggling to myself and placed a hand on my knee. "That's what I like to see. I love your smile," he spoke gently.

"Thank you."

"Ah yes, how can I—Mr. Hermes," the bank manager just knew he was about to get us right on up outta there until he realized who he was talking to. "I wasn't aware—Matilda didn't say it was you."

"All the more reason you should've got your ass out here before now. We been waiting a whole ass minute," Atif snapped. "My lady needs access to her safe deposit box, think you or a member of your inept staff can handle that?"

"I-I...uhmm, yes sir," he jumped and practically ran to a computer. "Mrs. Hermes, I assume?"

"Uhmm...Muhammed. Cary Muhammed."

"Cary...Cary...ah, here it is," he spoke shakily. "Cary Muhammed? Ahseir Muhammed's daughter?"

Here we go. "That's me."

"Your father was a fine man. A fine man indeed." The bank manager suddenly started kissing my ass like I was Jesus himself and he was trying to get through those pearly gates. "May I see you ID please?"

"Sure." I reached in my Fendi clutch and passed him my card.

"Everything appears to be in order. Follow me please."

We followed him back to the area where rows and rows of safe deposit boxes covered each wall in the space. The bank manager walked to the last row and opened the box in the middle with his key, waiting for me to use mine. Atif nodded and I inserted my key slowly as a feeling of dread washed over my spirit. The bank manager pulled the box out, placed it on the table in the middle of the floor and nodded to both of us before he quietly exited to give us some alone time.

"Atif, I don't want to know what's in here."

"Why not?"

"Something tells me there's something in here that I really don't want to know. Can we leave?"

"Baby, if you leave it here, you'll always wonder what's in that box. But if you're absolutely sure you don't want to know, we can put it back. Throw they key in the Atlantic Ocean and never talk about it again. Is that what you want?"

I stared at him for a second, pondering his words. At some point, curiosity would get the best of me and I would want to know, even if it killed me. "You're right."

"Open it."

I pulled the metal top off of the box and began examining the paperwork inside, getting angrier by the second. "Atif?"

"Yea."

"Who is Aram Hermes?"

"Pop. Why?"

"Why does my father owe him a half a million dollars?"

"Might have something to do with that house you own on Sunset Grove Lane," he replied lackadaisically. "He was supposed to sign it over to Pop after your stepmother started some shit in Chicago and my father took care of it, but when he didn't, Pop came out here looking for him."

"Then what happened?"

"Pop ran up on Juelz because your father implicated him too. At that time they had beef with some niggas from Iran and claimed they couldn't do nothing because the Iranians kept hitting up their stash houses. Now I know for a fact that had something to do with Juelz stupid ass, but Pop told them he'd take care of that too."

"I'm confused on what that had to do with my house though."

"I'm getting to that. Pop did what he had to do with the Iranians, then went back to Ahseir and Juelz and told them he needed his money. Juelz started talking 'bout he was supposed to do that, since he sold weapons to a lot of the gangs out here. Pop threatened to kill his ass, but Ahseir stepped in and was the peacemaker. He offered up the house—"

"Why MY house, though? My father had homes all over Florida!"

"Because that's the address Lenore wrote down as collateral when she got those pills from Pop in Chicago."

"What pills? Donnell sent her scripts—"

"Nah, Donnell couldn't send her the kind of work she needed up there," Atif schooled. "He would've lost his license if he was supplying her with perkies and addies like we was able to. What he sent her was for her personal stash, she was throwing pill parties and shit every other day! Plus she was well-connected in the film industry before she started fucking that producer, so she had to have something for that. Aye, that bitch was up there throwing raves and shit—"

"Ok, wait. My daddy could afford a half million dollars though."

"Nah…not after Pop gave him the terms of the loan. See, while he was taking care of the Iranians here, apparently Juelz got in Ahseir's ear and told him don't pay us shit. So, they thought they got away with us doing a hit plus getting Ahseir's hoe out of that little bind she got herself in when the gangstas up on the north side got a hold to her. They had her ass in a dumpster up off of Howard Street near the train, told that bitch they was gonna slit her throat if she ain't come up off the good dope!" he cackled.

"What?"

"Yea, she was trying to run off on them, trying to pass some aspirin off as them perkies," he cackled. "Anyway, Pop wasn't fronting her no work on consignment after that, she had to put something down just in case she tried to run off again. She gave him the house. Then when Pop came down here to collect, she disappeared. Pop showed up at y'all crib wanting his shit, Ahseir told him he had to talk to his business partner because he had part ownership—"

"Which was a lie!"

"Yea, we know. Like I said, Juelz started talking about the Iranians, we took care of that. But before he did, Pop made Ahseir sign a promissory note saying he was gonna give him the house, free and clear by a certain date. When he went beyond that date, interest started accruing at twelve percent every two weeks. Even after Ahseir died, that interest still accrued because he didn't own the house, you do."

"So, was this whole thing between me and you—"

"At first when Juelz called, yea. But then—"

"REALLY, ATIF? You got me all in over here and this was all for…what exactly? My house?"

"Nah, we don't want the house no more. Pop want his money. And since your father lied and said the house belonged to him and Juelz, he owe us too."

"How much does he owe you, Atif?"

"Cary, it don't matter—"

"HOW MUCH!"

"At the time of the original debt, the house was worth over $500,000. Considering the amount of time that has passed and ain't nobody came up off no coin, you looking at about—" he did some quick mental math in his head, "your father's half a million dollar debt has compounded to over twenty eight million dollars, give or take a few hundred thousand. So Ahseir owes us fourteen million."

"At least I'm worth something," I snickered crudely. "So, you want me to sell it or…"

"Cary, let's talk about this…"

"Atif, had you said something before we started this whole thing…" I started collecting all the paperwork together in a neat stack when my eyes landed on a birth certificate. Sliding the paper closer to me, I read over the words on the paper and froze in complete and utter shock. I had a sister. "Ain't this about a fucking BITCH!"

"What's wrong now?"

"Oh nothing." I replied bitterly while I stacked the papers on top of each other and shoved them inside the metal box, slamming the hinges shut. "I just have a whole ass sister out here that my father knew he went half on that I knew nothing about!"

"A sister?"

"Yea. And get this: he was even bold enough to bring the girl around me, neglecting to mention we were related!"

"Who is—"

"MYA! Mya is my sister!" I snatched my bag off the table and whipped out my phone to call an Uber.

"Cary, where you going?"

"Fuck you Atif! Fuck this bank, fuck a legacy…fuck all this shit! I'm LEAVING!"

Leonidas

I hated coming out to Coral Gables for anything, but this muthafucka Stan that we got our pistols from insisted we came to his spot instead of meeting up. Damn, I missed the good ol' days when Pop got his shit from Dom Killuminati up in Michigan, but he was supposedly a family man now. I still had his number, but shit, I could barely get him on the phone unless it involved the kind of money I didn't want to spend.

"Aye, Juelz ain't got no other connects? This the best he could do?" Duval grumbled once we stepped off the elevator. I ain't got no problem with nobody's sexuality, but damn. Put some clothes on when you know muthafuckas coming to yo' spot. No matter what time of day or night it was, this nigga walked around naked when he should've been handling business. Came to the door in a towel, but dropped it before he sat his naked ass, balls, and dick on the chairs. Said it was for our own protection, since he was the pistol man. We never sat down in his crib, either.

"Fucked up as it is, this nigga got the best prices on pistols, considering we need some untraceable shit," I frowned. "We only deal with him once every blue moon and now that's over with, so let's hit the block and see what's going on in the streets."

I shoved the entrance door out of my way so fast...I didn't want to be seen coming out of a building this man lived in. Everybody knew how he rocked. "Call Santiago and see...what's good, Duval?"

He stopped in the middle of the sidewalk, staring at something to my left side. "Aye, ain't that Cary standing on the curb?"

I squinted before looking in the direction he was pointing. "That's her. Where her little friend—"

She hopped in a black Benz truck and sped off as Atif rushed out of the building she was just standing in front of. "What's good, God? Or should I call you Atif?"

"Leonidas Payano," he stopped and snickered while rubbing his hands together. "What a coincidence. You gonna kill me now or later?"

"Aye, I ain't got no beef with you, Atif," I spoke sincerely, Maggie's words echoing through my mental. "If Cary chose you, that's something I'm gonna have to live with. Treat her right, aight?"

Atif gave me a quick once over before he seemed to focus on my words. "So I guess it's later then, huh."

"What?"

"Only a pussy ass hoe would threaten a man and try and take it back," he kissed his teeth and sized me up one more time. "Since you ain't upped strap, I'm looking forward to catching that bullet sometime later. In the meantime, this ain't a fuckin' peace treaty. Fuck outta my face with that 'treat her right' bullshit. I told you from jump to treasure your woman if you had a good one. You didn't, so here we are. At least be man enough to shoot me from the front, make sure I'm looking you head on when you kill me. That's how the G's do it, in case you didn't know." Before I got a chance to respond, he walked off, chuckling to himself.

"Damn, when we—" Duval turned in the direction Atif swaggered away from us.

"Aye, that's the last thing on my mind right now. We gotta find Lenore so I'll have a bargaining chip when I'm ready for her to come home."

"Lenore? You still ain't take care of that?"

"Can't find her." We made it to the parking lot where Duval's car was parked and got in. "A lot of shit hinging on her death right now."

"If you can't find her, how you know she ain't already dead?" Duval questioned before hitting the push button start on his whip.

"That's the thing: I don't know." I ran a hand down my face and sighed, the curve of Cary's ass as she stood on the curb burned in my memory. "We could be out here chasing a ghost for all we know. But until that ghost shows up, I'ma keep looking."

‡

"What he say?" Santiago called and told me he had some important information on Lenore and I was tuned all the way in.

"So apparently his cousin told him he was at work early one morning before the sun came up when he was on God's security detail." Santiago knew this one chick who was fucking this one dude who had a cousin who worked for Atif. "Said they grabbed a chick out the car butt naked, gave her some of that magnesium citrate, you know the shit they give you before surgery that makes you shit?"

"Yea."

"One bottle will have you shitting all day, but they made her drink three bottles, then tossed her in one of those big ass shipping containers. Said she had to be in there shitting her insides out, because as soon as it hit your system you can't hold it."

"Damn, straight up?"

"Yea. So God and Cary show up bout twelve, twelve thirty. By then the smell was so strong you could smell it outside of that muthafucka! Can you imagine shitting in the dark on a wood ass floor? Everything just melting together when the sun come up—"

"SANTIAGO!"

"Oh, my bad," he snickered. "Anyway, they show up, Cary go inside and say something to her while God told Buck to grab something from his truck. Buck go to the truck, only thing in there was this long, leather case on the third row. So he grabs that, takes it to God. God unzipped it in front of him and it's a fuckin' machete! He hands Buck the case and walked inside the container where Cary in there talking to Lenore. Said he heard Lenore scream, next thing he knew they was telling him to clean out the container."

"So Lenore—"

"They carried her out of that container in two industrial strength bags," Santiago continued. "One for her body, one for her head."

"Her head?" I thought about the day Cary had Kimoyrah straddled over the trough where Benny had the concrete mixed and ready to go. Kimoyrah was in mid scream when Cary swung the machete like A-Rod, severing her head from the rest of her body. Even laughed when it landed in the concrete and sunk to the bottom. When she told Maggie about it, auntie looked so proud…

"Her head, my nigga."

"Aight, good looking, Santiago." I hung up and sat back for a second to think. We been looking for this woman for two months and she been dead for a month and a half. Once again, I allowed somebody to do what I was supposed to be doing when it came to my woman.

I wasn't no bitch, but in hindsight, I probably shouldn't have threatened that man. He ain't did shit to me, and now he was looking for a gunfight. A man who rode around the city with machetes in the third row. All this was over some shit Pop was keeping tight lipped about for some odd reason. I had to get somebody on the phone that

I knew he wouldn't lie to, regardless of how the truth made him look.

The phone rang twice before going to voicemail. I hung up and called back to the same thing. On the third try, I got an answer. "Ma."

"What, Leonidas?" she snapped.

"Damn, that's how you answer the phone now? 'What'?" I snickered, trying to lighten the mood because she seemed irritated.

"You act like I'm out here sitting in the house with my thumb up my ass!" she sniped. "Talk quick, I'm busy!"

"Busy with who? I just passed yo' house and Pop's car outside!"

"None of your fuckin' business, dammit! I'ma ask you one more time what the hell you want before I hang up!"

"Lenore."

"What about her?"

"She dead."

"Ok, and? That's good."

"Ma, you—"

"Bye Leonidas!" she hung up before I could get a word out.

Every female in my life has lost they damn mind. I got up and went in the kitchen to find something to eat. Ma, Cary, Okeema, the twins…all of them was getting on my nerves and I ain't have the patience after fucking with Atif earlier.

Chapter 18

Cary

"It's about you! Cary, you losing yourself in this man—"
Yenni's words were on repeat in my head as I rode back to my house…Atif's house…the house I shared with my married boyfriend who saw me as nothing but a job. How could I have been so STUPID? This man only pursued me because he wanted to collect on a debt owed to his father. And Juelz actually sent this man TO MY HOUSE to what, kill me? Force me to sign over my property? My daddy's stupid ass allowed this to happen? Is that why he bought all that other shit and put it in my name, so he could hustle them out of their money by pretending like he was broke? For them to be these so-called smart ass dope boys, they were both as dumb as a box of rocks.

"Signed over my house because he wanted to save an ol' raggedy snatch bitch," I grumbled as we took the long way to my house on the Venetian Islands. On what planet does that make any sense? He should have just gave that man his money and been done with it.

Here I am thinking my daddy was the smartest man I knew, the brains behind the whole operation and come to find out this hoe Lenore might've been right when she said he owed her his whole empire. This bitch was a go-getter. Her friend steals her man, she kills her and gets him anyway. Yea, she had to put up with his kid, but that was a small price to pay considering what the end result was. She had access to all his money while he was alive, so she fucked that up for as long as she could, gets him to put his house up when she damn near put him in the poor house, then had him killed when she finally got sick of the bullshit.

Oh, but sis didn't stop there. She uses his name to keep getting work fronted to her, knowing he ran off on the plug twice. To keep breathing air, she goes and marries somebody else and builds up her customer base. Then, when these folks pop up in her home town and it's either run the bag or her life, she goes and kidnaps the kid that will get her debt erased. "Bravo, bitch."

"Excuse me?" the Uber driver questioned wearily.

"I was talking to myself."

"Oh." He turned the music back up slightly, nodding his head to the female voice singing over the pan flutes.

In the short time we knew each other, I developed strong feelings for Atif. My woman's intuition must've been broke, because when we first met I knew for a fact I wanted him. Whether it was temporary or permanent, I wanted to be lost in his hazel gray eyes, I wanted to be surrounded by his huge muscular arms, I wanted to be wrapped up in his aura like when he carried me out of my bedroom in my childhood home. I wanted to be in his orbit, the only planet circling his sun. And I got him too. But all that was before I discovered I was being played.

● ● ●

I dug in my purse and pulled out my phone. Scrolling through my contacts, I hit talk on his number. I had some questions and Atif was gonna talk to me, dammit.

"Cary."

"I just find it funny how—"

"How did you know where I live?"

"Excuse me?"

"My house. I'm following you on the FindMy app and you're around the corner from my house."

"What? I don't know—"

The truck pulled up in front of a gorgeous estate in Key Biscayne siting on the edge of the island with spectacular water views and less than a mile away from Juelz's home. "Excuse me—"

"Here's your destination, miss," the driver turned to me with a devious smirk. I just noticed his phone which would have displayed the address and the GPS location to my destination, was nowhere in sight. "Have a great day."

"This isn't where—"

"I do not speak English," he smirked, pointing towards the door. "Please get out of my truck."

"You sound like you speak English just fine muthafucka!" I screamed, raising a heeled sandal to kick him in the face before I heard Atif yelling on the phone. I forgot to hang up, and it was a good thing too.

"Atif! This crazy ass Uber—"

"Aye, Pop wanna see you. Get out the truck and I'm bout to pull up in a minute."

"Your—YOUR father?"

"Yea."

"Fuck you, Habibi!" I spat before doing as I was told. I thought his father was in Armenia with his wife, fuck he wanna see me for?

Atif pulled up and parked in front of me before he exited his truck. "Cary, I swear this wasn't supposed to—"

"What do you think you can say to me right now—"

"Look, I don't do the back and forth with nobody, not even my wife," he interjected. "So if you ain't gonna shut the fuck up and listen, you can walk yo' ass home!"

"I thought I was going home, but looks like I ain't! "Your family can't seem to—"

"Atif?" A woman met us at the gate as our voices echoed through the quiet neighborhood. "Is this her? Is this the woman you're leaving me for?"

"Royalty, go in the house. I'll be there in a minute."

"No, I wanna see what's so special about THIS woman that you'd walk away from five years with me and your daughter to be with her!" she gritted. "Hmph, you ain't that much younger than me, sis!"

"Royalty, I said—"

"This is a picture of our daughter," she ignored him and shoved her phone in my face. "She wakes up every morning to her daddy! Our sons," she flipped through the pictures of two teenagers and a little boy who was the spitting image of his father, only darker. He was too cute...and could high key pass for my son. "...who love their father more than anything! Do you know how it feels to be tossed in the trash for a newer model? You think he ain't gonna do the same thing to you when the next lil' chocolate thang switches her ass across his eyesight!"

"I didn't ask for this! I didn't tell your husband to divorce you! Wanna know what he told me? You was rebound pussy and he finally woke the fuck up! If anything the shoe is on the other foot, I had a man sucking my pussy every night! You know how many times I begged him to go home? Pleaded with him to go home to his wife, to his family? Your husband washes my panties and hangs them up to air dry, he wasn't trying to leave!"

Now Royalty trying to play me like I'm pussy. I ain't about to be keeping this man's secrets hoping he'd choose me when he had a whole ass family. Maybe I suggested that he divorce his wife if he wasn't happy, but it wasn't my fault he wasn't happy in the first place.

"Atif is that true? I was—you told this woman I was rebound pussy?" Royalty's eyes shone as she waited for his response.

"I mean, if you look at the timeline—" he shrugged his shoulders like it was nothing.

"So all those times you told me you loved me, that was just you out here taking advantage of the rebound?"

"Royalty, go in the house and—"

"And you brought the woman who you're leaving me for to the home we share...the home WE built—"

"Be clear: I bought this house before I married you," he interjected. "Don't start claiming shit—"

"Atif. Royalty. Cary." An older version of Atif popped up out of nowhere, I didn't see this man walk up. "Come inside."

"Papa, Atif—"

"NOW, Royalty."

Atif's wife turned on her heel and followed the older man with her head down. Atif reached for my arm and I pulled away, the sooner I got him out of my system the better off I would be. "I can't touch you, Cary?" His whisper came soft as his lips were when he planted kisses on those secret places of my body that only he knew. I was fighting a losing battle between my heart and my head the longer I was in this man's presence.

"Please don't."

"So it's please now, huh," he caressed his fingertips along my neck and across my shoulder, down my arm to rest on my hip.

"Atif, your wife is right there," I pointed just as she turned to see what was going on behind her back. "We not gonna do this right now."

"Can we do it later?" his voice dropped to that tone he had on the boat when we were about to— "Please?"

"Did you hear your wife?"

"Mmhmm." He nuzzled his face against my neck as soon as she dipped off into another room in the house. "I want you though."

"I can't. I told you that before, I can't." I pushed him away amid my body's pleas to give in to his whims.

Royalty appeared out of nowhere in front of us with a shotgun cradled in her arms as she dropped two in the chamber. "In my house, Atif? IN MY HOUSE! We can dead all this divorce shit right now! I'd rather be a widow than a fuckin' divorcee!"

Atif shoved me to the floor and dove in front of the gun as she perfected her aim. "I'll always love you, Cary," were the last words I heard before I closed my eyes, not wanting to see the man who loved me more than anyone, including my daddy, as he took his last breath.

"ROYALTY! NOOOO!"

Leonidas

Breaking news from Miami Beach: We are live on the scene as the police made a gruesome discovery only moments ago. A body belonging to...wait...they're bringing someone out now. As you can see, this was the scene of a heinous crime committed by criminals in this quiet community. We will bring you more details as this story unfolds. Back to you in the studio.

"Ain't that out here?" Killa stressed as he changed the TV to ESPN.

"Yea. That's fucked up, all these million dollar homes out here and niggas still getting bodied." *At least we got a spot in the everglades to drop these niggas off,* I snickered to myself.

Pop came downstairs looking suspect like a muthafucka. "King, when you get here?"

"Few minutes ago. Why, I can't come out here no more?"

"Nah, it ain't that, I'm saying though," he kept looking back and forth between me and the steps. "Call before you come, aight? Ain't no telling what might happen, I just so happened to hear voices down here and it's y'all. I thought somebody broke in."

"But you got a monitor in the office though."

"Yea, but I wasn't in the office."

"Aye, who you got upstairs?" Not only was Ma sounding suspect, so was he. Maybe she came home and they was trying to surprise a G.

"King, don't stress—"

I hopped up and went upstairs to see Ma. So much had gone on since she'd been gone and she was the only woman who gave me the kind of advice I needed. Maggie was too blunt, sometimes I wanna have a woman on my side to agree with me at least once before I got the 'but'. Sliding past Pop, I rushed up the steps and into his bedroom to see Okeema trying to cover herself up. "Oh, suck my dick and come fuck on Pops, huh. That's how the game go now?"

"I told you that day before I left somebody liked my pussy," she snickered. "Yo' mama ain't here and somebody gotta take care of a man of Juelz's caliber."

"Exactly what caliber is that, slimy bitch?" I seethed. "Too old to pull pussy on his own and too thirsty to not hit the same pussy as his son?"

"So you do care, huh King," she chided. "Aww, that's so sweet. Maybe I can tuck you in a few nights before I take care of my future husband."

"Bitch I don't live here. Tuck that nigga in!" I snapped. "By the way, I found ya auntie. The bitch dead. Guess who killed her?"

"I know who better not had—"

"She did. Didn't give a fuck about you or your feelings, took that bitch head smooth off!" I cackled. Okeema needed to let that marinate while she letting Pop blow her back out with what little strength he got. "Tuck that in, bitch. Keep giving Juelz that pity pussy, I'm straight."

Pop tried to stop me as I jogged down the steps to get the fuck out of that house. "King, I know you ain't mad—"

"Nah, go lay up with a hoe that's two years older than your daughters. I guess that's some hot shit to do, huh."

"King—"

"Y'all have fun. Don't let me interrupt. Oh yea, while you hitting that raw, Okeema got the clap, just so you know." I started church clapping as soon as I got to the front door. "That bitch a walking round of applause! AAAHHH!"

I chirped my new Audi and got in, checking my phone which had been vibrating like crazy:

Unknown number: *Leonidas*

Me: *Who dis*

Unknown number: *I'm sorry. I'm sorry for everything that went down between us*

Me: *WHO IS THIS?*

Unknown number: *Cary*

Me: Bullshit

Unknown number: Leonidas mwen renmen tout bagay ou fe mwen, ti bebe (I love everything you do to me, baby). Remember that?

Me: Where are you

Unknown number: I can't say. I just want to say I'm sorry

Me: Cary

Me: Cary

Me: CARY

I hit Jaden's line before I did anything. "Aye, can you do a reverse trace on text messages too?"

"A reverse trace? Hell naw nigga, you go to prison for that if you get caught!" he snickered.

"And you don't go to prison for hacking a muthafuckas security camera, huh? Ain't that an invasion of privacy?

"Yea, but you do twenty years for hacking the government."

"I need to know where she at, man. Y'all don't understand, I need that woman—"

"We got'chu, bro. Just not enough to be doing fed years, that's all."

"God's people would've done it, scary muthafucka."

"If they called my boss God, shit I would too," he snickered. "Don't get me wrong, King is cool, but we talking about an untouchable muthafucka."

"Fuck you, Jaden," I grumbled before I hung up. All these niggas pussy.

Okeema waved at me from my parent's bedroom window before she disappeared behind the curtains. My girl somewhere and I don't even know if she safe, Ma in California prolly fucking my new stepfather, and Okeema getting tore out the frame by my own father. "Fuck Miami. I'm bout to hop a flight."

Chapter 19

Cary

Where..."Where am I?"

"Safe."

"Where is 'safe'?"

"Here."

"But—"

"We won't allow anything to happen to you, Cary."

"Where is Atif?"

A long pause came before I was given an answer. "I'm right here, Cary."

"What? I thought—"

"My son's death will come long after I take my last breath," Aram Hermes appeared out of nowhere as my eyes adjusted to my surroundings. We were on a plane with nothing surrounding us but blue skies above and bluer water below. "Once you become a parent, you'll realize that."

"Can someone please tell me what happened?"

"Royalty tried to kill me and Pop shot her."

"What?"

"You want me to repeat it?"

"No. I'm saying though…" I tried hard to focus on the voices around me before I heard the gun go off:

"ROYALTY! NOOOO!" That was Mr. Hermes' voice.

"Atif you love her! You tell her you love her while I have a gun pointed at you!" That was Royalty.

"What you want me to say!" Atif roared…

"That you love me! I WANT YOU TO SAY YOU LOVE ME!"

"I DON'T! YOU DON'T GIVE A FUCK ABOUT ME!"

"We still could've made this work! What about our daughter! What about Armani?"

"Royalty put the gun down! Put the gun down!"

"NO! I don't give a damn if we hate each other! We'll always be together, Atif! In life and in—"

POP! POP! POP!

And that's when I passed out.

Leonidas crossed my mind and I sent him a text so he knew I was ok. I hadn't said a word to him since that night in front of the strip club, and at the very least I owed him an apology to cleanse my spirit. It wasn't for him and his shady ways, it was for ME so I could move on. "Where are we going?"

"I told you. Madagascar. They got some good food out there."

"Atif—"

"Me and you are nothing like me and Royalty. I swear—"

"I'll always have love for you, Atif. But I can't do this."

"Why not?" he tilted his head, a puzzled look spread across his features.

"I just—"

"Is it because I'm married?"

Do you know how it feels to be tossed in the trash for a newer model? You think he ain't gonna do the same thing to you when the next lil' chocolate thang switches her ass across his eyesight! "No."

"You don't love me."

"Atif, you have given me enough memories these past few months to last a lifetime. I just feel like those memories were all built on a lie."

He stared at me for a few minutes longer, lost in thought. "Pop."

"Yea son."

"Have the pilot turn the plane around."

"But we're halfway across the Atlantic—"

"Pop, I can't keep somebody who don't wanna be kept. Take us back to Miami."

Aram Hermes looked back and forth between me and his son before he took a deep breath in and blew it out. "Ok."

Leonidas

"Yea, so I'm bout to go down to Brazil and fuck with Alberto for a little while to get my head on straight," I stopped for a second to watch a chick with pretty brown skin walk by in a fluorescent orange bathing suit top with some blue jean cutoff shorts, ass bouncing like a basketball, before finishing my conversation with Kimbella. "Might be back in a week, might be back in a month, might not ever come back."

"You need something to get your mind back right," she agreed. "Cary getting kidnapped was some crazy shit, you ain't been right since."

"She did text me though. Said she was sorry for everything we went through."

"And?"

"I took that."

"You took that, huh." Kimbella's lips screwed up on the side of her face. "Did you give it back?"

"She stopped texting, so I figured she ain't want it back."

"Same selfish ass Leonidas. Yea, you do need to go somewhere and gather your entire life," she sneered.

"What I'm supposed to do about that? I can't make her text me back!"

"It's the thought, dummy! Whether she responded or not, apologize dammit! Sometimes you act like the sun shines out your fucking ass, I swear!"

As much as I didn't want to admit it, Kimbella was right. I owed Cary an apology at the very least, considering that my bullshit was the reason we weren't together:

Me: *I'm sorry*

"Sent it."

"Don't tell me, send it because it's the right thing to do! Damn, if it wasn't for the blood of Jesus I would've wrote you off as my brother a long time ago!" she snapped and hung up.

Shaking my head, I continued to walk through the airport until I saw a familiar face. Actually, two. "Ma? What you doing up here with Mya?"

"I went to pick your mother up from California," Mya fidgeted, looking like she wanted to jump out of her skin.

"She grown. My mama ain't need you to come pick her up." Now I was confused, Ma and Mya was cool?

"Hey baby, I got the passes—Leonidas?"

"Ahseir?"

Ma straight faced me as he walked up and wrapped an arm around her waist. "Son, we need to talk—"

• • •
21

Chapter 20

Cary

"Can I at least take you home?"

"That's how we got in trouble the first time," I snickered sadly to myself.

All I wanted out of life was to love and be loved. I didn't need the money, the fame, the whole 'princess and queen' titles. I just wanted to be genuinely loved by a man and give that same love back. Leonidas was a distraction from Tony, but Atif…God, Atif made my body shake in ways I didn't know were possible. And as if that wasn't enough, we could talk about nothing for hours with our clothes on. He comforted me during a rough patch in my life and stayed afterwards. I think I was the one who allowed him to truly grieve his second wife and get past her death. And for all that I had…nothing.

"Cary—"

"Atif, please." His name on my lips still made my thighs squeeze together knowing him as intimately as I did. His intimate lips when they meshed against my intimate places with a gentleness that only he could give. How my right leg would bounce with anticipation when he would look at me intimately from across the table. How intimate our lovemaking was…how he could go for hours literally BEGGING for one more taste of my coconut cream…

"What we gonna do about the house?"

"What house?"

"The one you living in."

He took me to my childhood home to grab the money from the closet. After I bagged up all $2.5 million of those dollars in fifties and hundreds, we brought it back to our house, spread it out all over the bed, and made love on the pieces of green paper with Benjamin Franklin and Alexander Hamilton's faces sternly admonishing us for fucking on their faces. Atif was so attentive to my needs that night... "I don't care. Sell it. Keep it. Doesn't matter."

Atif kept watching me for some odd reason and the way his hazel gray orbs reflected not the sunny day that it was in the city, but a cloudy haze had me about to say fuck it and let the chips fall where they may. I had to be strong. For all women who fell in love with the wrong man, I had to be strong. "Call me if you need anything. I know you said you never wanna see me again, but—"

"Deleting your number as soon as my Uber pulls up."

"Are you gonna keep the car?"

The day he bought me that car, he drove while I sat in his lap bouncing up and down on his thick pole while we cruised through the city behind tinted windows on our way to the airport. Each time we stopped at a red light, Atif held my shoulders down and shoved his dick deep inside my pussy while tonguing me down. This man

• • •
21

was an expert at giving me back to back orgasms, his stroke game made me want to give him and only him the pussy. Everything about that Porsche reminded me of him…"No."

"So you just gonna erase me completely out of your life? We never happened?"

I fought the tears threatening to fall down my cheeks as I checked the Uber app, willing the wetness to halt. "We happened."

"We happened, but I can't say goodbye?"

I remembered when he said hello…hearing his strong, self-assured voice as he called up the steps when I thought I was dead. The twinkle in his eyes that only came about when he was amused or being his masculine self. The way he would drag his tongue across the back of my neck while we were… "It's better this way," I squeaked.

Atif moved from my right side to standing behind me, close enough for me to feel the heat from his body, yet far enough for us to not accidentally touch. "Better this way, huh. Is this what you really want, Cary?"

No. "Yes."

The white Mercedes pulled up at the same time as a commotion came from the entrance to the airport. Heads turned in the direction of where two male voices bellowed expletives at each other as a familiar woman's voice screamed for them to stop. "Oh my God. OH MY GOD!"

"What's wrong, baby?" Atif immediately jumped to my defense, shielding me from any violence that might break out. I prayed that the scuffle between the two men right before my eyes was my imagination, or even a cruel joke that wasn't funny.

"That's…"

Atif turned to the spot I couldn't tear my eyes away from, even if I wanted to. "Leonidas? Who is that he arguing with?"

"My…my…"

Atif had me cradled in his arms before my legs gave away completely. "Cary, baby tell me what's wrong."

"Atif, that man is my father," I whispered, as if Ahseir could hear me.

"I thought your father was dead."

"I did too…"

"I love you, Daddy. I'll always love you." I leaned in and planted a kiss above the bullet wound that took his life before whispering in his ear. "And I promise I'll get that bitch for taking you from me if it's the last thing I do." All these years…all that I'd been through in my lifetime and he wasn't dead? And why was Aunt Judy and Mya out here with him?

The white Mercedes pulled off as Atif pressed his lips against my forehead, a touch that I felt from him so many times before. Here was where I felt safe, right or wrong here was where I belonged, in his arms. My father faked his death and was out here arguing with Leonidas about I don't know and don't care what. His loyalty was to me as his daughter, oldest, youngest, none of that shit mattered. Yet Mya was here and so was Auntie Judy. *So she knew too. All that 'Cary is my baby' shit and she knew.*

"I'm taking you home." Atif's voice filtered through the roaring sounds in my ear and in my head. What were these people shielding me from because everything that they'd done had already come to the light. Plus I was older and nothing surprised me anymore.

"Where is that?"

"Our house."

"But—"

"No buts. Let me take care of you, Cary."

I was tired. Tired of being lied to, tired of being cheated on, and tired of fighting with the world for a piece of happiness in it. Tucking my head in the crook of his neck, I closed my eyes and the commotion around me faded away replaced by the heartbeat of this man. "Ok."

Leonidas

"My mama? You fucking my mama, Ahseir!"

"Leonidas, listen—" Ma pleaded with tears streaming down her pretty, gingerbread tinted skin. "We didn't do this to hurt you!"

"Why the fuck did you do it, then!" I snapped. "My whole life…all I heard about was what a great man you WERE, and now I find out you got my mama stretched out in Cali?"

Ahseir reached out to put a hand on my shoulder,, but I swatted that shit like the zika virus. "Leonidas, we didn't want you to know yet—"

"YET? Fuck you mean yet!"

"Son—"

"Fuck you doing out here, Mya!" I turned my attention to her scared face.. "Something you wanna tell me too?"

"Uhmm…"

"Nah, we out here having family reunions at the airport and shit! How do you fit in to our little group of incest!" I spat venomously.

"King, we're not related—" Ma tried her soothing voice, but for something like this, that wasn't gonna work.

Mya kept fidgeting with her fingers, as if she was debating on whether to speak now or forever hold her peace. "Me and Juelz—"

"Excuse me?" Ma's ears perked up at that one. "You and Juelz what?"

"Nothing." Mya started speed walking to the exit doors, determined to get the hell away from us.

"Mya! Mya come back here! You can't do that! You can't bring up my husband's name—"

"Oh, so now he's your husband?" Ahseir wanted to know. "Just a few hours ago you said he wasn't shit to you!"

I looked back and forth between my mother and Cary's father, wondering how long they been fucking. If anybody should want Pop dead it should be me. Only female I had that he hadn't hit or tried to hit was Cary. Sometimes I used to wonder if him and Miranda had something going on, even though she wasn't old enough to consent. "Ma, why?"

"King, yuh just don' know what ya fadder 'as done to me!" she cried out in her thick Caribbean accent while stuck between the entrance and the exit.

"So that's the reason you and the Walking Dead over here creeping around the country!" I roared, not trying to hear the bullshit. "You got this man's daughter in yo' house—wait, that's why you always calling her your daughter? 'My baby Cary', this and 'Leave my daughter alone' that?" All this time I thought she made those comments because of how close our families used to be, now

I'm finding out her and Ahseir were actually smashing? I had to get away from Miami. I had to get the fuck away from Miami.

"King listen—" Ahseir's voice came from behind me as I sped out the exit doors.

"You know how many nights your daughter cried herself to sleep in my arms because of you? How many times she woke up screaming in a cold sweat because she had another nightmare about when she was raped as a kid? All this and you—"

"JUELZ RAPED ME!" Mya yelled. "He used to touch me when I was eight years old! He made me put my mouth on him! He used to—"

Ma walked up out of nowhere and slapped Mya so hard I got dizzy watching her collect her bearings. "Stop saying those tings about me husband, gyal! We 'ave ah set of twin gyals dat he neva touch!"

"I—I—I'm sorry," she whispered, holding her face. "I—I gotta get out of here…"

"Judy what the hell was that?" Ahseir gave her the ugliest frown before he ran off behind her.

"Ahseir! I'm sorry! AHSEIR!" she screamed as she ran off behind him.

I stood and watched the unlikely couple, still confused as ever, but by this time not really giving a fuck enough to follow them. I had a ticket to Brasilia and a checked bag on Delta. "Lemme get the hell outta here for real," I mumbled to myself as I went back inside. Brazil was gonna see me.

Chapter 21

Cary

"Tellin' me this, tellin' me that…let's do a sixty-nine…"

"Come get this tongue…so I can kiss that lil' pussy til it's numb—"

It had been a few days since that incident at the airport, and life was finally returning to some normalcy. Per usual, Atif was somewhere in the house remixing Teyana Taylor's new song and doing a horrible job at it. "Who you doing all that to?"

He popped his head in my bedroom from the hallway with a sneaky smile spread across his face. "You."

We weren't even sleeping in the same room, but my body knew he was somewhere close. If I had a vibrator, that muthafucka would be dead by now. "Nuh-uhn. We are friends in every aspect of the word." I pulled the yellow satin sheets up closer to my chin. "We ain't making no cancer signs tonight, tomorrow, or the next day. I ain't the six and you ain't the nine."

"You look like a cake sitting in the middle of that bed," he smirked, walking inside the room before taking a seat on the edge of the mattress, tugging at the sheet. "Yellow on top, sweet, sweet chocolate in the middle—,"

"Atif, stoooop," I didn't know how long I could go on resisting the memories when he was right here in front of me ready to make more.

"You got that shit I'm cravin," he sang off key, rubbing my naked thighs through the sheer material. "And I want you to sit on my face...you gonna give it to me?"

"Atif—"

"Cause you waaaaant it—"

"No I don't..."

"Lemme make your toes curl one last time and I promise I'll leave."

I don't want you to leave. "You promise?"

"Mmhmm." He locked eyes with me while one hand kept sliding the sheet up inch by inch. Smirking devilishly, he dove under the covers where I ain't have no panties on.

"Atif we can't keep...ooohhh, God," I moaned as my eyes rolled in the back of my head. "Yes...yes...yes..."

"I don't wanna leave you Cary, but I know we ain't gonna ever be like we was," he mumbled to my coochie. Atif kissed my shaved mound before he slid his fingers between the wet crevice of my love. Delicately spreading my muff open, he slid his tongue slowly back and forth from my clit to my slit. "I'll always love you. Always."

"How…mmm…why? Why couldn't…ooohhh…"

"I love all the women who gave me a baby," He lifted my legs up and turned me into a human peace sign before diving off the deep end to splash in my womanly waters. "You want a boy or a girl?"

"Atif, I'm not…mmm…I'm not—"

"I know your body, Cary. Yo' lil' pussy always been wet, but this girl right here got the God all up and through her, don't she baby?" he spoke to my clit before tapping the tip of his tongue in the puddle between my slit.

"Ooohhh…can I…can I…"

"You wanna cum one last time for the God? Give it to me," his moans were so fuckin' sexy, "Put that sweet cream right where it belongs, baby."

"AAAHHH!" No man had ever made me squirt as hard as he did, and I doubted it would ever happen with that amount of intensity after him. "Baby—"

Before I knew it, Atif's tongue was in my mouth, swishing my sweetness against my taste buds. This…I was gonna miss his lips pressed against mine, the slight breath he inhaled before the low growl while his wet beard hair brushed against the top of my naked breasts. His hands roaming indolently over my skin before he took my nipple between two fingers and squeezed while he adjusted his girth to slide in my…

● ● ●

"Mmpfh…Atif…" I half moaned, half whimpered once he found his way inside. I loved it when he took my left leg and cradled it in the crook of his arm, still with his tongue in my mouth as he tried to climb inside my womb with his stroke. I wrapped my arms around his broad, strong back and squeeze him closer, try to pull him in…we both mashed our faces in the crook of each other's necks as he fucked me better than I'd ever been fucked in the past.

"Do you love me, Cary?"

"Atif—"

"Tell me. Do you love me?"

"Yes…oh yes. I love you Atif."

"How much?"

How was I supposed to answer that? "I love you, Atif."

"Have my baby. Come with me…shit, this pussy good like a muthafucka…come with me back to my homeland and have my baby. Please Cary."

"I…" I didn't know if he wanted an answer or not, but I was beginning to feel that tickle that started at the bottom of my spine and moved around to my pussy before it spread to the rest of my body.

"Cary."

"I'm about to—"

Atif abruptly slid out of me and hovered his thick dick covered in my juices just out of my reach. "You gonna answer me or you gonna cum first?"

"What the…" I tried to take care of myself, but he was quicker, pinning my hands down on the mattress. "ATIF!"

"ANSWER ME, CARY!"

"Answer you? What—" He asked a question? Damn, what did he say? "Uhmm…what?"

"Yes or no?"

"Yes or no what?"

"Just go with whatever comes up first."

If I said yes, it could be something I would've normally said no to. If I said no, it might be something that I might end up dead behind. I knew how he rocked. "Yes."

"Come catch this nut then," he palmed that anaconda between his legs and tugged him back and forth a few times.

I was the one squirming like an earthworm, but now I had to catch something for him? What about me? "Boy fuck you."

"I was just fucking with you. Come get cleaned up," he snickered playfully, climbing out of my king sized bed and heading to the shower.

"See, that's why I can't stand you now, always playing," I slapped his outstretched hand away from me. "You play too much." I giggled.

"Let's play target practice, I'm 'bout to pin yo' ass up on the shower stall and shoot these missiles all up in yo' lil' box for a lil' while," he cheesed playfully. We were all set to get in the shower when something tripped the alarm. "The fuck?"

"Atif—"

"Stay right here baby, I'll be right back." He grabbed his robe from the back of the bathroom door and walked through the bedroom to investigate. I didn't know what was going on, not too many people had this address. Hopefully it was nothing, but…

"The fuck is you doing at this house?" Atif's voice came from the living room.

"Aye, tell Cary the King sends his condolences," Killa's voice came out of nowhere before I heard something that made my blood run cold in my veins. POP! POP! POP!

I dropped to my knees hearing that all too familiar sound pop off just a few feet away from where I shook in shock. My body let out a gut wrenching scream before I fell completely to the floor in tears. "NOOOOO!!"

Leonidas

Me and Alberto sat and politicked for a little while as the hoes swam back and forth in the pool. Life was good in Brasilia, and I had no plans to go back home soon. I spoke a little of the language, just enough to say, 'let's fuck' and 'money' in Spanish. *Puta* and *dinero* were both universal, regardless of where I went.

"Aye, Estevan said he talked to your sister today. You should give her a call," cuzo spoke with his eyes tighter than fish pussy.

"So she can tell me to come home? Nah fuck that. They started that shit show up there, let them finish it." I took another hit off the gas as two of the hoes swam to the pool to get another hit of the Brazilian fish scale. "I'm good."

"You don't think they miss you? What about *tu madre, amigo*?"

"Fuck her too," I griped. "How you gonna tell somebody about what they shouldn't be doing when you doing the same shit?"

"Do as I say and not as I do," Alberto chuckled as he passed me the blunt. "Parents the masterminds of that shit."

Cary crossed my mind for some odd reason, but I shook it off. "Yea, that's why I ain't having no kids. Too much of a headache."

An unknown number popped up on my phone's screen, and I hit the talk button before I put it on speaker. "Yea."

"LEONIDAS! WHERE ARE YOU!" Cary screamed in my ear.

"Around, why?"

"GET YOUR ASS BACK TO MIAMI! YOU HEAR ME! GET YOUR ASS BACK TO MIAMI RIGHT NOW, DAMMIT!"

"FUCK YOU CARY! YO' SHIT AIN'T MY PROBLEM NO MORE!"

"Do you know what you've done? DO YOU KNOW WHAT THE FUCK YOU'VE DONE!" she wailed hysterically in my ear.

I hung up on her ass. Talmbout 'do I know what I did'. What the fuck have I done and I'm all the way in Brazil? Just in case she decided she wanna call again, I switched my phone to do not disturb and went back to blowing that good green with my new potnas.

Cary

No…no…no…I couldn't…I couldn't go into that living room and see him like that. Death followed him wherever he went, but this…no.

On my hands and knees I crawled into my bedroom and searched frantically for my phone. The sirens in the distance alerted me that my neighbors already called the police, but…Atif…no…

I hit talk on the number of the only person who could have possibly been responsible for this. After all, he threatened him weeks ago, and Atif told me he'd bumped into Leonidas the other day. I know he wasn't still upset because we didn't work out…

"LEONIDAS! WHERE ARE YOU!" I screamed when he finally answered the phone.

"Around, why?"

"GET YOUR ASS BACK TO MIAMI! YOU HEAR ME! GET YOUR ASS BACK TO MIAMI RIGHT NOW, DAMMIT!" Why…why would he do that to Atif?

"FUCK YOU CARY! YO' SHIT AIN'T MY PROBLEM NO MORE!"

"Do you know what you've done? DO YOU KNOW WHAT THE FUCK YOU'VE DONE!"

"MIAMI P.D.! Is there anyone in this house!" someone yelled after Leonidas hung up on me. Clutching the phone to my chest, I sat on the floor and sobbed as the officers rushed my bedroom pointing guns in my face.

"Please...please check...please save him! SAVE HIM PLEASE!"

"If you're talking about the man on the floor in your living room, ma'am I'm sorry but he's deceased," a female officer informed curtly. "Now, you wanna tell us what happened? Starting with why you're in this house?"

"This is my home," I sniffed, trying to stand, but gave up when I couldn't. "My boyfriend and I—"

The male officer pulled a small notepad from his tight uniform and licked the tip of the pen before he began scribbling notes. "And what's your name?"

"Cary," I sniffed. Finally wobbling to my feet, I leaned on the wall for support. "Cary Muhammed. Like I was saying, my boyfriend—"

"What's your boyfriend's name, ma'am?" the male officer interrupted again.

"Atif," I sniffed. "His name is Atif—"

"Hermes? Atif Hermes?" both officers exchanged worried glances before they turned back to me.

"Why..."

"Atif Hermes was here? Ma'am, this is important…"

"Why are you talking about him like he's not dead on my living room floor!" I snapped. Who was in charge of the police academy, because these muthafuckas were dumb as hell.

"Because he isn't. Now we're gonna have to take you down to the station to ask you a few…ma'am are you ok? Paul catch her before she…" was the last thing I heard before I fainted.

Chapter 22

Ahseir

I was laid up in the Fontainebleau hotel and Judy didn't seem to be in any rush to tell her people I was back. Truth be told, me either, but I had to see my princess. I went up to the bank the other day and they told me she'd been there, so I knew on top of faking my own death, there was a lot of other shit I had to answer for.

First and foremost though, if you looked in the dictionary to find the definition of an ain't shit nigga, that was definitely me back in the day. We was making so much money that I didn't give a damn who I got pussy from, long as I got it. Christina was the first good girl I hit off because everybody else: Lenore, Judy, Mya's mother Taylor…all of them popped that pussy like Khia told them to on that one track. Judy and Taylor weren't strippers, but Lenore? Man…half of Miami ran through that shit like an Olympian by the time I got it. She was the piece that was accessible when my baby mama died, so I made sure it stayed there.

Taylor used to let me slide in them guts while her nigga was on the block working for me. I'd have him go all the way up to Hialeah for nothing while I put his girl on her head for 'bout an hour. Had her laid across the mattress looking like a sniper when she sucked me up and would dangle her over the edge when I would hit that pussy. She used to love that shit. Then when she got pregnant, I found out first. We had him thinking that girl was his when she looked more and more like Cary the older she got. When it came to pussy, these niggas dumb. Donnell was so dumb he even went and signed the birth certificate.

Judy found out about her husband and my hoe, so she came to the spot to confront him only to run into lil' ol' me. I knew what they were doing, but since I had Christina I didn't care. She ran up on me one night at this food spot after that, and I suggested she do the same thing he was doing. There was no point in her sitting at home waiting for him to come home because he was cheating, she may as well had.

I had been in contact with Aram through Judy, and he told me don't worry about that debt we owed. Bullshit aside, only reason he didn't kill us a long time ago was because he had me on a payment plan. Once I read over the terms of that loan, I knew I was gonna disappear soon and needed the money in Cary's closet to do so. So I transferred all my shit to my daughter's name and was supposed to grab it when I went out for a 'drink' that I wasn't coming back from. My mans Suso already gave me the lick about how Lenore hired him to kill me, so I was gonna hide out for a few days then pop up on her egotistical ass when she least expected it.

This hoe moved up the date, so Suso used a rubber bullet when he shot at me. Lenore must've had her own pistol because she definitely killed him. After my people at the coroner's office came through to pick me up, they dropped me off at an undisclosed location where I was supposed to lay low for a while. Dade County issued a death certificate for me, so I couldn't go to DCF and tell them to give me my baby back. Me being stupid didn't think anything would happen to her, after all Lenore always told her she would always be her mommy since her real one was gone. Even though they bumped heads a lot, Cary took that to heart. And then when it didn't play out like that, I know it crushed her soul.

With the rigorous training Maggie put her through, I couldn't believe it when I found out somebody touched my princess. Between my two daughters, Cary was the oldest and the most spoiled. I schooled my baby girl with as much knowledge as I could before I left so I would feel comfortable leaving her around other people. Finding out some sick fuck put hands on my baby…that shit damn near killed me.

I tried as best as I could to keep up with Cary, even when she worked the truck stops, but after that girl got killed I had to get out of Miami. Too much death in the city, and most of these girls were barely twenty-five years old. I moved out to Cali and settled in a small town right outside of San Diego, so if push came to shove I'd just go to Mexico and live out my life.

Then there was the small matter of Mya blurting out the name of a man who I trusted above everything else…a man who I called my brother as the person who did all the same things to her. Did this nigga who I used to trust with the only female who truly had my whole heart…was this muthafucka out here touching my babies and sticking his—I'ma kill his ass. I don't give a damn who he married to, I'ma kill his ass.

My phone dinged in my pocket and I pulled it out to check to see who was texting me:

> *Judy Booty: Baby, do you accept my apology?*
>
> *Me: You talked to your husband yet?*
>
> *Judy Booty: No*
>
> *Me: That's ya answer, love. I'm bout to hop a flight*
>
> *Judy Booty: NO! Come over, we'll get this straightened out*
>
> *Me: Nah, I'll pass. Call me when you get yo' life together*
>
> *Judy Booty: So you leaving*
>
> *Me: Yea*
>
> *Judy Booty: What about Cary*

I stared at those words with no response. What about Cary. How can I pop back up from the dead and tell my princess that I've been alive all this time and didn't reach out because I wanted to be selfish? And after what Leonidas said to me in the airport, my selfishness came at the cost of her individuality, her childhood, and her sanity. My baby was broken and it wasn't a damn thing I could do about it but blame myself.

• • •

Mya knew of me, but she didn't know I was her father. That was a conversation that needed to be had between Donnell and Taylor first. But I had caught her staring at me intently on more than one occasion when she came to Cali. Judy told her to come, that was another reason I kept her close all these years: she knew my secrets. And according to her, there was one more that she had and planned on telling me once we got back to Miami. Since that hadn't happened, fuck her with her big booty, Belizean ass.

Judy Booty: *Aram Hermes just called. Said he needs to see you immediately*

Shit. Now on top of everything else I had to hear his fucking mouth.

Me: *Aight*

I took a quick shower and put on a suit and tie. When Mr. Untouchable called, you betta have yo' ass suited and booted to go holla at the real king. Aram Hermes was a man who was on the level everybody wanted to be on, but couldn't because he was already there. There was only one reason why he called: either somebody was dead or somebody was about to die. Debating on whether or not I needed to make peace with my daughter before I went to see him, I decided to pop up on her once I finished handling business. It had already been twenty years, a few more hours wouldn't hurt.

Cary

"Ma'am, you do understand the severity of these charges, correct?"

I sat and stared at the pasty-faced detective, mouth set to hush mode.

"We can hold you for up to seventy-two hours if we want. Seventy-two hours. You wanna stay in holding or you wanna go home? Your choice. You wanna stay or you wanna go home?"

The Latina sitting across from me was playing that 'good-cop-bad-cop' bullshit, but I couldn't tell which one was the good cop because they both sucked.

"All you gotta do is tell me a story. One little story and this'll all be over. Just like those stories on the Kindle. You read e-books, Cary?"

Blank stare.

"Don't tell these guys, but I like Fatima Munroe. Girl, it was something about that Married To A Chicago Bully series that did something to me! You like Fatima Munroe, Cary?"

I wasn't gonna allow her to make me hate my favorite author, but this bitch was definitely pushing it. Me and Atif read that one novella, Taste by Fatima, and he been sucking my pussy like Thad did Lyrica on the side of the road ever since. I was thinking about submitting my own story on the website, especially since I saw they were accepting new authors.

The lady cop was laying it on thick with that whole 'identify with the perp' shit she probably learned from watching Law and Order SVU. "Cary, this won't end well for you—"

"Listen dammit, Atif Hermes is a dangerous man! And if you know where he is or where he hangs out and you aren't telling us, we'll throw your black ass in jail for the rest of your fucking life!" the white man banged his fist on the table and glared at me.

No this nigga didn't just— "Are you done?"

"Hey, ready to talk?" the lady cop smiled politely.

"Yea. My lawyer is gonna eat your bitch ass for breakfast," I glared at the male detective through tight slits as I spoke pointedly, "and fuck you in the ass before he throws you off of one of these bridges out here, hoe. Now be a dear and get me a phone so I can call him up."

"You ain't—"

"And on top of this pussy ass interrogation, you deny me of my right to an attorney? Not to mention neither of you jackasses told me I was under arrest, but yet here we are. By the way, I find it funny how I'm not in trouble, yet Dick Tracey over here talking about how serious some charges are. AND nobody read me my Miranda rights. Where's the chief?"

"I—" The female detective had to be new, all that pseudo-macho infusing the air around her was starting to make her act crack. "You have the right—"

"Nah, too late, bih! Get me a phone so I can go!" I sniped. Only reason I sat in the station house for so long was because I didn't want to go back home. Flashbacks of Killa laying flat on his face dead would haunt me for the rest of my life. Killa was a good dude, but Leonidas shouldn't have sent him to my house to kill Atif. Now I was being interrogated about his whereabouts as if I actually knew where the hell he was. If I knew that, I'd be somewhere getting nailed to the cross like he always did when we took a shower together.

They jumped like the pigs they were when that tap came on the door though. The lady cop went to the door and whispered back and forth with whoever before she came back in the interrogation room. "Our apologies, Cary. You're free to go."

"Damn right I'm free to fuckin' go, I ain't the criminal in here," I grumbled on my way out.

"Can you contact us if Atif—" the male cop wasn't that dumb. HE COULDN'T BE THAT DUMB.

"Fuck you Chuck and Lupé! *¡No dejes que te atrape sin esa placa, los jodo a todos!* (Don't let me catch you without that badge, I'ma fuck y'all up!)"

• • •
24

"Try it, mami," the lady cop jumped first, like I wouldn't beat the fuck outta her outside of this building. "I guarantee you'll be spending the night in lockup!"

"Mmhmm. *Sabes dónde vivo, para que te levantes* (You know where I live, pull up)," I smirked, strolling out of the interrogation room. I stopped off in front of the desk sergeant to check my phone and heard the voice of the last person I expected to see here or anywhere else.

"Cary. I know this must come as a shock to you, but—" Ahseir Muhammed began with his hands outstretched in my direction for a hug. *Daddy* was a term reserved for the man who acted like one, not this scary ass nigga standing in front of me.

"Pardon my back, SIR." I purposely bumped into him and moved around. Seriously, he couldn't have thought this whole thing through. Twenty fucking years had passed since I saw his face in a body bag. IN A BODY BAG. He didn't whisper to me that he wasn't really dead, didn't send a message, nothing. I'm positive if Juelz knew where I was, he did too.

"Cary Muhammed! I'm your father!" Ahseir roared at my back, causing a scene in the middle of the police station. "Don't—"

"Right. DON'T." I glared at him maliciously. "DON'T try to be a father now after twenty years! DON'T think you gonna come back and I'm gonna run in your arms crying about how much I missed you! DON'T come trying to save the day after all I've been through WITHOUT YOU! You damn right, DON'T!"

"Cary, I—" he dropped his head looking for an ounce of sympathy that I just didn't have to give, "I didn't know…can we go somewhere and talk about this? Just me and you?"

I shot him a sideways glance, taking note of the tailored suit and tie that hugged his body perfectly. The diamond cufflinks at his wrists and the corner of a handkerchief tucked neatly in his suit pocket. The fresh flower neatly pinned to his lapel that matched the silk tie adorning his neck. While I was selling pussy to survive at the truck stop…while I was in a state where I knew absolutely NOBODY that could come save me, I did things that STILL made me cringe when I looked at myself in the mirror. And through all that, Ahseir Muhammed obviously hadn't missed a night of sleep worried about my safety. "A wise man once told me that he wanted me to stop being small. Outgrow the spaces where my comfort has held me stagnant. To level up unapologetically."

"I don't think I ever said that to you—"

"You're right. You didn't. Atif did. And it's a damn shame how a married man who everybody felt like I should stay away from can give me so much game for free. You know I realized something these past couple of months."

"What's that?" Ahseir sneered. SNEERED. As if he was taunting me. As if another man couldn't have possibly taught me more than that little shit he did.

"All this time I've been looking for someone to replace YOU in my life. All this time, I've been looking for a man who had the same traits as YOU. Not knowing that YOU were the thing I needed to be protected from in my head. Looking for you had me stagnant, stuck in my childhood looking for someone to protect me. But now," I chuckled when his face dropped in embarrassment, "now I know why Auntie Maggie gave me all that training. Now I know what she meant when she told me what she did," I nodded, finally understanding. It wasn't Leonidas. It was never Leonidas.

"What did she say?" Ahseir asked with anger stewing just beyond his furrowed brows.

"She said I would know I was with the right person when I looked at him. When I got that feeling of appreciation and respect when I was in his airspace. When I could control my patience with him. When I could have a conversation with him about nothing and feel he was the only person I could trust with my secrets. When I was with him and I could be me, but he encouraged me to be the better version of me. You never taught me that."

"We didn't have enough time—"

"The time was there. YOU weren't. Goodbye Ahseir. Do what you do best: disappear."

"Cary, please!"

I stared in those brown eyes that were identical to mine for the last time before I left him standing in the middle of the station house. It was time for Cary to love on Cary.

My head was pounding after all that crying from seeing Killa dead in my house. From the way it sounded in my bedroom, I really thought it was Atif. The thought of someone having to plan his funeral knowing he had no family to bury him…that made my chest hurt. Since it was gonna take my Uber twenty minutes to get to the police station, I ignored my inner voice and sent Yenni a text to have his body cremated. Five minutes later, my phone was ringing with her number.

"Hello."

"Cary, I'm sorry I said those things to you," Yenni rushed. "I was—"

"You know what I found out during this whole back and forth thing between me and you?"

"Sis, it's really not that deep—"

"Bitches be secretly feeling some type of way the whole time they fuck with you. Let y'all have a small disagreement and they suddenly telling you how they feel about you for real. You could've said all that shit while we were still good."

"Cary, I didn't mean—"

● ● ●

"Me and you ain't the same, sis," I gritted. "I mean, me and Leonidas was good when we were, but now we ain't. You talking bout my house and it ain't did shit to you, sis. I didn't lose myself in Atif, I know exactly who I am. But you though? You was so hungry for love from a man that you settled for the crumbs Bash gave you. You were so desperate to avoid being lonely that you accepted disappointing love from a disappointing person. You threw away your standards just to have somebody…anybody love you to the point that now you feel lonelier than ever. You couldn't just be happy to see me happy, nah I had to be a dick gobbling hoe."

"It was never my job to wait for Leonidas to get his shit together and act right. He needed to come correct or get replaced, and that's what happened. Now you in a place where you have no idea on how to function with the information given to you and I feel bad for you. I really do. But had you kept your mouth shut, we could've got through this together. Sorry can't fix us, Yenni. Make sure somebody goes and grabs Killa from the morgue or they'll put him in a pine box. Goodbye. SIS."

I hung up without waiting to hear her response. Damn it felt good to be freed of all that pent up negative energy.

Chapter 23

Cary

A few months later

"Bring me that baby!" Philomené yelled across our yard. "It's time for my grandbaby to eat something!"

"Ma, I'm tired of eating," I grumbled, wobbling to where she stood in the doorway with arms outstretched for a hug. "My feet swole, plus the doctor said they gonna put me on bedrest if I keep gaining weight like this."

"Good," Atif chuckled, rounding the corner. "Then I won't be worried about you falling down when you go to the market. You nine months pregnant, you know," he traced the stretch marks on my belly with care before leaning down to kiss my belly button.

"You can't keep me hostage like this. I have rights too," I giggled, touching a hand to his face when he came back up.

"Mmhmm. You got all the rights in the world, Mrs. Hermes."

"Both of y'all and y'all 'rights' better get y'all asses to this table and eat, I know that!" Atif's mother fussed. "My grandbaby is starving!"

We both bussed out laughing as we followed her inside of the Mediterranean-style villa that sat on the edge of Lake Sevan. The water was gorgeous throughout the day, but when that sun set…Atif could've got me pregnant all over again and I wouldn't have minded not one bit. "I'm glad we decided to stay here, because that house y'all got in Ararat was a hot mess," I giggled.

"It wasn't like that when I was growing up." Atif used to speak so fondly of his childhood home on those midnight cruises back in Miami that I couldn't wait to see it. Yea, when we got here I found out I could've waited a couple more years. "Pop let the house fall into ruin like that, hopping continents every couple of months."

"Yea, yea, whatever. We sold it didn't we?" Papa Hermes snickered, probably thinking back to the day when he called a truce and sold Ahseir and Juelz that house that was crumbling down around itself for the same money they owed him. Dumb asses.

Jacari and Jacoby plopped down at the table and dug into their food while Atif Jr. and Armani continued playing outside. "Boys! Did you wash your hands before you sat down at this table?" Mama fussed about everything, and it was so funny.

"Gramma, we—"

"Get to that sink before I take off my belt!" she snapped, knowing she didn't have a belt to take off and even if she did, she wasn't gonna do nothing with it. "Y'all know better than that!"

"Yes ma'am," they both grumbled as Jacoby took one last bite of his food.

"This what you gonna have to deal with for the next eighteen years with these Hermes babies!" she playfully rolled her eyes at her grandsons. "Spoiled as hell! Atif got these kids rotten!"

"Mama, leave my kids alone. They just being kids," he spoke softly, holding a strawberry to my lips. "Open your mouth, baby."

Those four words coming out of his lips was an instant pussy wetter for me, but I clinched my legs together and did as I was told. Rubbing the sweet berry against my bottom lip first, he leaned in as I flicked my tongue out and we crushed the fruit together between our kiss, Atif licked the corner of my mouth as he came up for air. "Mmm…"

"Taste just like you," he moaned with a smile.

"Cary, I almost forgot to tell you, a letter came for you today," Mama went to grab the FedEx envelope off the table in the foyer and handed it to me.

"Who is that from?" Atif questioned with a raised eyebrow.

I turned the envelope over a few times before I stared at the return address. "Oh, it's from Mya. We met up before I left and I gave her the address out here. Remember I told you, love?"

"Yea I remember, but I still don't know whether I can trust her or not," Atif tugged at his beard, lost in thought. "Why didn't she just call?"

"Remember you changed my number and told me don't give it out after Yenni kept playing on my phone?"

"You right. What she want, a place to stay?"

"I don't know, lemme see." I opened the envelope as Papa Hermes and Atif's phones both buzzed urgently at the same time.

"Babe, I'll be right back, aight?" My husband pecked the top of my head before he and his father rushed off to another corner of the house.

"Atif! Armani! Come in this house!" I vaguely heard Mama yell as I read my sister's words spread out across the wide ruled paper:

Cary,

I've always cherished the bond we had, ever since we were kids growing up. After all that we've been through together, who knew you were my sister? Damn, it's crazy how our lives mirrored each other's so much and we didn't realize it.

You were right about Ahseir. He ain't nothing but a self-serving asshole that was more worried about that money than he was about you. I couldn't imagine growing up in a house with a man who led you to believe he loved you, cared about you, and had the audacity to call you princess, knowing he didn't give a fuck. Because if he did, like you said, he wouldn't have left you the way he did. Especially not with Lenore. Now on that part, I was glad he left me with

● ● ●
24

Donnell, because that's who really treated me like a princess after he finished med school.

But that thing with Juelz haunted me down to my soul. After we talked that day, I sat back and thought about all those times he did what he did to me. I thought about all those times I would spaz out on people for no reason, and come to find out I just wanted to be heard. Can you believe that even after I did like you suggested and went to their house, Judy STILL didn't believe me? It wasn't until Ahseir came in and started digging in her shit did she finally realize I was telling the truth. Now what if he wasn't there. That island bitch would still be calling me a lyin' ass gyal.

Speaking of which, guess what. Kimbella and Kourtne'a are our sisters too. Bitch, why Judy lied and told Juelz Ahseir raped her? And why everybody knew the truth about the twins BUT Ahseir? Can you believe these two old muthafuckas was tussling over that geriatric hoe, but when it came down to him touching me, Ahseir ain't really have too much to say to that man. Like I said, a waste of fucking life. Then Juelz gonna call me up talking about 'can we meet up at the pier so he can apologize the right way.' I had to get away from them people.

I heard Leonidas and Okeema had that baby. Reason I say Leonidas is because they got that DNA test done and guess who the pappy was. Yea, he walking round Miami looking siiiiick! And every time I see him I ask if he talked to you. I know that nigga be ready to kill me! I don't know what happened, but Juelz ain't top dog in

Miami no more and he big mad about it. Serves his ass right, all the shit he done did to people and got away with. Fuck that whole family.

Reason I'm writing you this letter though is because King got it in his head that you belong to him. Bitch, he be at the club popping off about how he still owe your husband a bullet for taking you from him and another one for murdering Killian. Said some crazy shit about how cheating is a part of a relationship, and every man is supposed to hurt you. Yenni cussed him out, because you know her and Bash ain't together no more since he couldn't keep his dick in his pants. King told her she stupid because Bash was that man worth her hurting for and she should've fought for her relationship to work. He was in the hospital for a week after she broke a bottle of Louie the 13th across his skull.

Me and Benny was talking about it the other night, and he agreed that I should reach out to you. I'm praying this letter gets to you before King takes that flight, because his parents moved over there to some village that starts with an A. I hope that's not close to you because—

"Atif! ATIF!"

"Cary, baby what's wrong?" Mama Hermes ran into the kitchen where I was frozen in shock from Mya's words. "What does that letter say?"

King said he's coming to take what's rightfully his. And he don't give a fuck who gotta die in order for him to have YOU.

BOOM! BOOM! BOOM!

"Ma! Take Cary and the kids underground!" my husband yelled as footsteps rushed across the rooftop. "NOW!"

"Come on, Cary! We gotta get you and this baby down these steps safe, my son would have a fit if..."

"I told you I was coming back for my bitch, didn't I!" Leonidas's voice came from the front of the house as Mama swung the iron door behind the cupboard closed.

"Mama, wait—"

"Cary, Atif said—"

"NO! I can't leave him again! I can't—" I stood on the top step bawling my eyes out. My first baby, a man who loved and cherished me, and I was gonna lose him to Leonidas? My ex might still actually have love for me, but I doubted he was IN love. He probably still thought about me all the time, but he didn't do anything about it but hop a plane to Brazil from what I heard. Leonidas was shit-faced about the fact that Atif was the man who made it obvious that he wanted me in his life, and that wasn't from sexing me everyday. And now I was supposed to lose that happiness because of this conceited, gaslighting asshole?

I pushed the door opened a crack and what I saw made me wish I hadn't. Ahseir, the man who went half of me was laid out in front of the cupboard with his insides completely filleted like a fish while gunshots continued to ring out as if I was in the middle of a firing squad. "ATIF!"

One of the men who walked the rooftop on security detail appeared out of nowhere and gave me a light shove back behind the steel door. I sat at the top of the steps, unable to move while hot tears of remorse rolled down my cheeks. *Please,* I begged to whoever answered prayers. *Please let him be safe. Please,* I whispered over and over as my body rocked back and forth, panicked.

"Cary, come downstairs with me and the kids," Mama Hermes tried her best, but I wasn't budging.

"Mama, I gotta know he's safe. I gotta know he's ok."

"Cary—"

"Oh God," the puddle of goo easing from between my legs was enough to kick in my motherly instinct, even though I had no idea of what the hell I was doing. "Mama, I need him, please go get him, I need him, please!" I couldn't do this without Atif. He promised I wouldn't do this without him.

"Baby, you can do this. I made him and I'm here," Mama gave me the scolding I needed, because I was slowly unraveling. "You are a Hermes woman and dammit we ain't no bitches! Come on so we can get my grandbaby out!"

I tried inching down the steps as best as I could, considering every time I moved, it felt like the baby shifted. Suddenly the door to the basement creaked open and someone sighed behind my head. *God, please don't let this be Leonidas.*

"Where this puddle of water come from?" Atif questioned calmly. "Cary, you wasn't gonna tell me my baby coming?"

"I—AAAHHH!"

Atif jogged down the three steps and swooped me off my feet, carrying me upstairs to the bathroom. He tiptoed through the bodies of the dead, still laid out with blood seeping from their open wounds. I saw Leonidas near the steps and truthfully felt nothing, not even remorse at the fact that he died with his eyes open. "You ain't gonna make it to the hospital. Lucky for you, I've done this a few times."

"I was so worried—"

"Why?"

"It was so much going on…I thought—"

"What?"

"I thought I lost you." I laid my head on his shoulder and inhaled the scent of gunpowder mixed in with his Hermes cologne.

"Know what's funny?"

"What's—oh God, I'm having another contraction—"

"Breathe through it, love," he coached as we took cleansing breaths together. Mama was already running water in the jacuzzi by the time we made it upstairs. "Good?"

"Good."

"Now, like I was saying: know what's funny?"

"What?"

"I saw you chop a woman's whole head off, yet you worried about me," he snickered.

"That's different."

"How is it different, beautiful?" Atif soothed, lowering me down carefully into the water.

"That was about survival."

"And this wasn't?"

"Well—"

"Feels good to be a woman for a change, doesn't it?"

"I'm a woman all the time, what you mean?"

"I'm not saying you ain't." Atif gently pulled the maxi dress over my head and slid off my panties. "What I'm saying is that when a woman is with the right man, it's easy. Your feminine energy flows naturally, you can be soft. None of that masculine energy you had to have with ol' boy because he wanted to play that Bonnie and Clyde shit." His hands gently kneading my shoulders were the relaxing touch I needed to get me through the throbbing pain of pushing a whole human from my body. "You ain't have to worry about me, I told you I got you. That's that masculine energy feeding off of your feminine. Has nothing to do with that…what you call me that one time?"

"I said you have a hero complex…OOOUUU, these contractions coming closer together—"

"I'm your strength, just breathe through it," Atif puffed right along with me until the pain subsided. "Like I said, feel good to be a woman for a change, don't it."

Per usual, Atif was right. I wasn't the 'queen' that Leonidas and his people were constantly labeling me as. Yea, I knew how to shoot and do everything the boys did, but that wasn't my place. After all I'd gone through, at this stage in my life what I needed was a partner that wanted to be with me, not me and somebody else to have sex with when I wouldn't do what they wanted. Someone who had my back everywhere, not just the streets. Somebody that would go to war for me. Seeing Leonidas, Juelz, Ahseir and Judy laid out all over the first floor of my house, I knew I had that someone. "It does."

"You know what, Cary?"

"What?" I wheezed as I felt the beginnings of another contraction.

He stared at me lovingly even though I knew I had the ugliest frown in the world on my face. "You really have my whole heart. All of it. And I don't want it back, you can keep it."

"You have mine…AAAHHHH! ATIF!"

"Come on baby, time to push that baby out!" Mama Hermes wiped the tears rolling down her face before she sprang into action. "One! Two! PUSH!"

"AAAHHH!" my husband and I screamed together as I damn near crushed his hand. A loud plop landed in the water and my body felt empty in the place where I felt nothing but movement and love for the past nine months.

"IT'S A GIRL!" Mama cheered loudly. "Aram, it's a girl!"

"Come get me when y'all get the baby cleaned up, I don't wanna see all that!" he yelled from the other room.

"It's a girl, daddy," I smiled as Mama laid the baby on my naked chest. "What do you wanna name her?"

"Baby, don't be mad, but—"

I already knew what he was gonna say. "It's perfect. Kapri Ahmari Hermes." As a woman who was completely secure in her relationship, the fact that he named our daughter after his second wife didn't bother me.

His lips were perfect against my cheek, and I felt nothing but joy and peace. "I love you so much."

"I love you too."

The End

I'm not done, though. Keep scrolling.

A Note from Fatima

What a ride! Cary had me worried for a second there, but everything worked out in the end. Everybody loved Leonidas, but men do tend to show you their best side while the relationship is new. Give it a couple of months and good or bad, you'll find out who he is for real.

I know there was a lot of discussion around the fact that Atif was a married man, and regardless of what was going on with him and his wife, Cary should have respected that. Keep in mind, she tried on multiple occasions to send that man home. But I did give y'all a hint in the synopsis: what's a man to do when he's tasked with the decision to stay with the rebound chick or follow his heart. Should he have stayed with Royalty, knowing that wasn't where he wanted to be because they were married? And even when he tried to divorce her, she still refused to let go? Who's to say who's right and who's wrong? Y'all let me know in the reviews (and be nice. Amazon won't let y'all cuss, come to the inbox and do all that. But still leave a review).

#ISaidWhatISaid – NO SPINOFFS! This series ended exactly as it should have, and I was able to show respect to the G.O.A.T.s from the Married To A Chicago Bully series, which is where Atif came from originally.

Next from me: Be on the lookout for Pursuing Stormi-A Vampire's Tale, and also Enigmatic which will not release to Amazon. I'm not posting the synopsis, but here's a quick blurb:

Charming, yet mysterious. Everything about Channing was charming, yet mysterious. The way he walked. The way he talked. The way his fingers would 'accidentally' brush up against mine when we were alone. The way he locked eyes with me and smiled before mashing his lips against my palpitating nub. Sloshing his tongue around my most secret of places, there was an air of excitement when we snuck off to his car in the middle of our shift. There was something so...dangerous. Something so risky. Something so...enigmatic when it came to me and him...

Follow me on social media!

FB: http://facebook.com/authorfatimamunroe

http://facebook.com/monreauxpublications

http://facebook.com/groups/ReadingWithFatima

IG: http://instagram.com/fatima_munroe

http://instagram.com/monreaux_publications

Twitter: http://twitter.com/fatima_munroe

LinkedIn: linkedin.com/in/monreauxpublications

Website: http://fatimasbooks.com

http://monreauxpublications.com

Keep scrolling to see what's next from Monreaux

Publications!

Close your eyes trust me...

Coming Soon

Subscribe to our mailing list: www.monreauxpublications.c

9 798665 343815